MW01257837

In dedication to the memory of Bob, the father,
And the splendour of the indigenous Peoples of the Americas.

DOCTOR WHO
ATTACK OF THE
CYBERMEN

Based on the BBC television series by Paula Moore by arrangement with BBC Books, a division of BBC Enterprises Ltd

ERIC SAWARD

Number 138 in the
Target Doctor Who Library

A TARGET BOOK
published by
the Paperback Division of
W.H. ALLEN & Co. Plc

A Target Book
Published in 1989
By the Paperback Division of
W. H. Allen & Co. Plc
Sekforde House, 175/9 St John Street
London, EC1V 4LL

Novelisation copyright © Eric Saward, 1989
Original script copyright © Paula Moore 1985
'Doctor Who' series copyright © British Broadcasting Corporation,
1985, 1989

The BBC producer of *Attack of the Cybermen* was
John Nathan-Turner
The director was Matthew Robinson
The role of the Doctor was played by Colin Baker

Printed in Great Britain by
Cox & Wyman Ltd, Reading

ISBN 0 426 20290 2

CONTENTS

1

The Day Begins

Outside, the rain rained. It had been doing so all night. A rather effeminate man on breakfast television warned of continued inclemency.

'If you're going out t'day,' called a concerned mother, 'you'd better take an umbrella.'

The words of advice, mingled with the smells of breakfast, coasted up the stairs and into her son's bedroom.

'Sure, Ma,' he muttered, and pulled the sheet around his head.

Charlie Griffiths only ever felt really secure when he was warm and snug in bed. Yet he knew he must get up. Today was important. And he wished it weren't. He didn't like rainy days. Things always seemed to go wrong for him when the streets were wet. Especially when crime was planned.

'Breakfast's ready, son.'

'Sure, Ma.'

Whenever Charlie's Ma said that something was ready, he knew he had another ten minutes. She liked to give him plenty of warning, for Charlie moved very slowly first thing in the morning. She also knew he appreciated such small, caring gestures. It was one of the reasons why, at thirty-five, he still lived at home.

So instead of getting up, Charlie turned over and stared at the rain-streaked window. Somewhere in the distance he heard the time-pips on a radio.

It was nine o'clock.

As Charlie watched two raindrops race each other down the window pane, the door of his bedroom eased open. Silently, a small, black shadow stealthily entered, then raced across the open space to the bed and jumped onto it.

'Hallo,' said Charlie, lifting the sheet and allowing the cat to enter his safe, snug world. The creature purred loudly, which made him feel good.

Charles Windsor Griffiths had been named after the Queen's eldest son. There the similarity ended. Although his Ma had worked hard to provide him with the material comforts of life, circumstance had connived against her. Lacking a resident father to boost the family income, Charlie had decided, at a very early age, to subsidise his mother's meagre earnings with a little, gentle shop-lifting. At first he had been successful, but his lack of imagination (he always robbed the same department store) soon led to his capture. At the age of eleven Charles Windsor Griffiths became a convicted criminal. At twenty-one, a criminal psychologist declared he was a recidivist. By the time he was thirty-two, he had spent eight years and seven months in prison. It seemed likely that he would continue to spend the rest of his life in and out of gaol.

But then he met Mr Lytton.

And his luck changed.

Overnight Charlie became a success. Gone were the days when he would be picked up within hours of committing a crime. Gone too were the months, while waiting for the next job to come along, of living on nothing but Social Security payments and loans from his Ma. Nowadays Charlie received a good salary plus a bonus after each successful heist. Not only did he have money saved, expensive clothes, and a flash car, but he had also developed a sense of self-respect and purpose he had never experienced before.

Yet in spite of all this, the answer to one fundamental question still haunted him: why had Lytton employed him in the first place?

He knew that he was loyal and dependable, a valued commodity in criminal circles, but he was also aware of his many limitations, especially the 'loser' tag which years of imprisonment had earned him. With Lytton's proven ability to organise and execute daring crimes, he could have had the pick of London's best villains. Charlie knew this, which only added to his determination to learn the truth, whatever the cost to his ego.

'Breakfast's on the table, son.'

'Sure, Ma.'

Charlie sat up and stretched. As he did, the cat popped her head from under the sheet and scowled.

'Gotta get up, kitten. You heard what Ma said.'

Gracelessly he threw back the duvet and scrambled out of bed. A moment later he was half-heartedly engaged in his usual warm-up exercises. With the ritual completed, he picked up the crumpled heap that was his dressing-gown and shuffled over to the window. Outside, the grey street was enlivened by the presence of a red double-decker bus which had paused to pick up several bedraggled passengers. As it pulled away, Charlie watched a corpulent, middle-aged man, his arms waving frantically, run from a house further up the road. As the bus drew level it braked and the fat man clambered gratefully on board. Cheered by this small act of kindness, Charlie suddenly felt better about the day.

In spite of the rain, he decided, it might not be such a bad one after all.

A dark blue Granada turned into Milton Avenue and pulled up outside number thirty-five. Impatiently the driver sounded the horn, then lit a cigarette. His name was Joe Payne and he was also a member of Lytton's team.

Although it was only ten o'clock, Joe was already halfway through his second packet of cigarettes. This wasn't unusual. In fact, such was his huge consumption of tobacco, he had earned himself the nickname of 'Coffin Nail Joe'. Even without the ever-present cigarette, the all-year-round ebony tan sported on the index and third fingers of his right hand bore witness to his habit.

Joe was not a healthy man.

The horn sounded again.

This time the ground floor net curtains of number thirty-five were drawn back and Charlie, now dressed in jeans and a black polo neck, appeared at the window holding a piece of toast heaped high with marmalade. This he waved in greeting before stuffing it greedily into his mouth.

Joe scowled. He didn't like Charlie very much. But then he didn't really like anyone.

Not even himself.

Unlike Charlie, Joe had never been to prison, even though the activities of his small backstreet garage were not always within the limits of the law. Whether a car was legal or stolen, Joe could always cope. A quick respray for a doubtful BMW, changing a Jag's chassis and engine numbers, or running an oily rag over a legitimate ten-thousand-mile service, they were all in a day's work.

The horn sounded yet again.

This time the front door opened and Charlie, now clad in a smart black leather jacket and muffler, stepped out. Behind him came his mother carrying a multi-coloured golf umbrella. Although Joe couldn't hear what was said, it was obvious from Charlie's embarrassed expression that it was being insisted he took the umbrella with him. But instead of accepting it, and quickly getting into the car, he had started to argue, gesturing wildly at the sky, trying to convince his mother that it had stopped raining. These antics disturbed Joe as they were now attracting the amused attention of passers-by.

Quickly he lowered the front passenger-door window. 'Are you gonna muck about all day?' His tone was harsh and unfriendly, but it had the desired effect.

Charlie kissed his mother on the cheek, refused the umbrella for the last time and clambered into the car.

'That was not wise, Charlie,' muttered Joe, engaging first gear. 'It's not good to draw attention to yourself when you're on a job.'

As the car moved off, Charlie's mother waved farewell. Her son, acutely embarrassed, decided not to reciprocate. He knew what Joe had said was true. Anonymity was vital to the successful criminal. He also knew he couldn't afford to compound an indiscretion by agreeing. As the muscleman of the team, he had learned that it was more expedient to hide signs of frailty. So instead of attempting to excuse what had happened, Charlie adopted what he considered was a suitably macho expression, and to the sound of the car's ticking indicator, gazed silently out of the window.

Cautiously, the Granada turned out of Milton Avenue and into slow-moving traffic. Joe cursed at the delay, but Charlie didn't hear, so intent was he on watching Mr Patel, the owner of his local supermarket, purposefully making his way towards the bank. Charlie wondered how much cash he was carrying in the plastic bag clutched protectively to his chest and whether he made the same journey at a similar time each morning. Charlie would have to have a word with him. Warn him of his folly. As his Ma was an active member of the local Neighbourhood Watch, Charlie felt it was his duty to do so. He didn't want some part-time thug mugging the owner of his mother's favourite shop.

Once free of the jam, Joe accelerated hard.

'What's the hurry?'

'Nine minutes behind schedule. And Russell doesn't like to be kept waiting.'

Charlie let out a grunt of indifference. He didn't like Vincent Russell. There was something about his aloof, slightly stiff manner that was unpleasantly familiar, almost like that of certain policemen he had known. When Charlie had mentioned his suspicion to Mr Lytton, he had been harshly told to put such stupidity out of his mind. This only made Charlie more determined to learn the truth. If Russell were a policeman, he had considered, why didn't Lytton want to know?

It was this and other problems that occupied Charlie's

12

mind as the car sped along the road. Although he didn't know it at the time, they were really quite trivial to those he was about to face.

Although Lytton and his team had been active for two years, such was their success that the police had remained ignorant of the identities. This would have continued to be the case if they hadn't broken into an electronics factory engaged in highly secret work for the government and stolen part of a working prototype used to transmit light in a pre-calculated arc – in other words a machine which could generate a curved laser beam.

At the time neither Griffiths nor Payne had seen the point of this robbery. To them, real swag would always remain hard, instantly negotiable commodities such as gold, diamonds or bank notes. Stealing what seemed like nothing more than a few printed circuits could never excite in quite the same way. Still, neither man had complained, especially after the generosity of their bonus.

Although there wasn't any doubt in Special Branch's mind that the robbery had been carried out with skill, they were puzzled that the whole machine hadn't been stolen, especially as the time wasted dismantling it increased the chance of the thief's capture. Amazement soon followed as they discovered how brilliantly the factory's internal security systems had been neutralised. Such was the attendant praise of the perpetrator's skill, there was serious talk, once he had been found, of the factory employing rather than prosecuting him.

But in spite of Lytton's brilliance, he had made one vital mistake: he had not supervised closely enough Joe Payne's part in the robbery. Instead of providing an anonymous vehicle, Joe had stupidly supplied one from his own garage. He couldn't see the point of stealing a car which, after being used to transport them to the factory, would spend the duration of the robbery parked safely in a side-street half a mile away. But then Joe hadn't taken into consideration Lytton's final precautionary procedure of always reconnoitring the surrounding streets of an imminent robbery. He hadn't reckoned, as they cruised past the factory gates for the third time, that their presence would be recorded on video tape by a security camera.

Once Joe's careless mistake had been discovered, it didn't take the police long to trace the vehicle's registration, or for them to establish that the owner was incapable of executing such a robbery. Apart from lacking the necessary technical knowledge, Joe also lacked the style for such a crime. Whereas he might be capable of fencing a few stolen cars without getting caught, *real* master criminals would not risk their freedom by making the foolish mistake he had. Neither would they embroider their error by offering for sale, in their own garage, a vehicle used in a robbery. But there it was, parked on his forecourt, adorned with its 'Bargin of the Week' poster, for both punter and police to view.

The police placed Joe under close surveillance in the hope he would lead them to the organising brain. Since this led only to Charlie Griffiths, they began to fear they had made a terrible mistake.

Neither did the discovery of Lytton help much. Unlike the others, he was unknown to them. Yet when they made general inquiries, in an attempt to build a dossier of background information, they couldn't find anything. No one seemed to know where he had come from, who his parents were, or even where he lived. In fact, the more the police searched, the less they discovered. Nothing seemed to be known about him. Not even a birth certificate could be found. At the Department of Health and Social Security it was established he had never registered with a doctor, been admitted to a hospital, or purchased a National Insurance stamp. Even Her Majesty's Inspector of Taxes had never heard of him, which upset him greatly.

Deciding Lytton must be foreign, although his north London accent seemed to deny this, the police involved Interpol but they, too, proved unsuccessful in tracing Lytton's origins.

It was as though Lytton had never existed. The police became mesmerised which led them to make many mistakes. If only they had allowed their investigation to reach its natural conclusion, they would have learned that Lytton, in spite of his accent, was not from the planet Earth. But in 1985 the apparent was not yet acceptable, as contact with other life-forms had yet to occur. So instead they invented the hypothesis, which only further obscured the truth, that somehow Lytton had managed to slip through the bureaucratic net. But such was the improbability, no one really believed it, not even the police themselves.

When it came to the more temporal consideration of Lytton's criminal activities, commonsense, along with normal police procedure, was again abandoned, especially when they learned that he was no longer stealing electronic equipment but was now attempting to buy it. Instead of arresting and forcing the truth out of him (or even increasing surveillance) the police, in the hope it would speed up their inquiries, provided him with a supplier of their own, Vincent Russell. This only confused matters further: from the first moment of contact, Lytton seemed to know who Russell was and why Russell was there. Neither did it help their investigation when Lytton started to make outrageous demands, which both Russell and his back-up team were hard-pushed to satisfy.

It was only the news of the impending robbery which alleviated the police's sense of panic. They needed to arrest Lytton soon. Deputy Assistant Commissioners were demanding it. But they still hadn't solved the mystery of who he was. With this urgency in mind, and against the earnest advice of the Bomb Squad, it was agreed to supply Lytton with seven kilos of plastic explosives. Such was their desperation, it was provided without even knowing the venue of the robbery. At long last, they thought, the mystery of the 'Unknown Man' would be solved.

Instead, when everything went wrong, all it initiated was the biggest internal investigation the Metropolitan Police had ever known.

The car carrying Payne and Grifiths pulled up outside Fulham Broadway Underground station. As it did so, Vincent Russell stepped from its portals and climbed inside. A moment later the vehicle rejoined the main stream of traffic, this time on its way to collect Mr Lytton.

Commander Gustave Lytton came from the planet Vita Fifteen, in the star system Tempest Dine. He had been trapped on Earth for two years and was now desperate to escape. Lytton hated London with its teeming population, dreadful weather, dull conversation and awful food. As a mercenary soldier, he continually craved excitment. Robbing banks, with their ridiculously simple security systems, was not a satisfactory substitute for the bone-crushing rough and tumble of a good intergalactic war. But escape was impossible from a planet which had yet to invent the warp engine. The primitive spacecraft of Earth was useless. Even with his advanced technical knowledge, there was little he could do to improve the performance of such a craft. Not that it would have mattered if he could: Earth was too far from the main space lines. Without warp power it would take a thousand years to reach the nearest.

It had all seemed hopeless, until Lytton had hit on the idea of building a distress beacon. If he couldn't reach the space lanes, his signal might bring someone in search of him.

To use a conventional Earth transmitter, with its signal restricted to the speed of light, would have been as pointless as trying to escape from the planet. But with the adapted use of the stolen laser machine, and some half-remembered lectures on the structure of time, it was just possible to transmit a signal through the gaps in the space/time continuum. This would allow his transmission to speed across the Universe and, hopefully, into the receiver of a friendly listener.

This Lytton had done. What was more, he had had a reply.

Spots of rain began to pepper its windscreen as the Granada turned into Great Russell Street. Ahead stood the British Museum, its colonnaded front crowded with people.

'This is where we pick up Mr Lytton,' muttered Joe nervously. And as though to emphasise the drama of the situation, he drove his finger into the dashboard lighter and lit another cigarette.

As the car approached the entrance to the British Museum, an earnest-looking school teacher, hand erect in the 'Halt' position, stepped onto the pedestrian crossing. The Granada braked gently and the trio watched a gaggle of young school children, like so many nervous ducklings, scurry across the road. No sooner had her charges reached the safety of the museum gates, than the teacher thanked the waiting drivers with a stiff, formal smile before joining them. Joe engaged first gear, and as he was about to release the handbrake, the back passenger door was snatched open and Lytton got into the car. 'Hatton Garden,' he said, as though curtly addressing a taxi driver. Nobody spoke as the car moved off, not even to say good morning. Each member of the team was aware of Lytton's spiky moods and knew, on such occasions, not to bother him.

The drive to Hatton Garden was slow and tedious. The traffic was heavy and its movement sluggish. The car's noisy windscreen wiper sounded exaggerated in the tense silence. Neither was the atmosphere helped by Joe's chain-smoking. This had reached horrendous proportions as he now seemed to smoke a whole cigarette in two or three enormous inhalations, then immediately light another the moment it was finished. At one stage, Charlie was convinced he was actually smoking two at once, but as the visibility inside the car had become so poor, he assumed it must be an illusion. Quickly, Charlie fumbled for the electric switch on his door and lowered the window a few inches. Cool, moist air flooded in.

Although the four men now breathed a little easier, still no one spoke. When they finally reached Hatton Garden, the silence continued until they had driven the length of the road several times.

Then suddenly it was over.

'There you are, gentlemen . . .' said Lytton, indicating a dull grey tower block ahead of them. 'Ten million pounds.'

As the car drew level with the building, each man strained to read the nameplate alongside the main entrance: The London Diamond Exchange.

Joe Payne and Charlie Griffiths exchanged a quick glance. They couldn't believe what was being proposed.

'Very tasty,' cooed Payne at last.

'Oh, yes, very tasty,' echoed Griffiths.

Russell remained silent.

'Nothing to say?' inquired Lytton.

Russell stroked his upper lip. 'Not really,' he said at last. 'Not until I know how you're planning to get in.'

Lytton smiled. 'You'll see . . .' Then before any more questions could be asked, he ordered Payne to drive to Farringdon Road.

The mood in the car was now bright and cheerful. Things were beginning to happen. Already Griffiths and Payne, in their imagination, had started to spend their share of the money. Even Russell was excited by the idea of the robbery. For him it meant the conclusion to weeks of exhaustive work. Soon the mystery concerning Lytton would be solved.

At least that's what he thought.

As the Granada entered Farringdon Road, Lytton ordered Joe to cruise slowly. Satisfied that they weren't being followed, he indicated that they should turn left and they found themselves in a well-kept residential road lined with Victorian terraced houses.

Payne continued to drive until they came to a cul-de-sac, which they entered, stopping outside a boarded-up car repair shop. All but Payne quickly clambered out of the vehicle. 'Loose it,' muttered Lytton, banging the roof with the flat of his hand.

Charlie felt uneasy not having a convenient set of wheels, but no one was listening to him complain. Instead Lytton unlocked the heavy padlock on the garage door, entered the gloomy workshop and switched on the light. This seemed to make little difference, as its tiny output was swallowed by the black, copious oil stains covering the floor.

Neither did the place smell very nice.

Casting a last worried glance after the disappearing Granada, Charlie followed Russell into the workshop. The combination of gloom and dirt had an instant and depressing effect on their mood. It was as though the building was telling them it was old and tired and had been neglected for too long.

Charlie glanced around the workshop. To one side was an old fashioned mechanic's inspection pit covered by a row of wooden railway sleepers. Next to it was a tidy pile of clay and soil, as though someone had been excavating. At the far end of the room was an extendable, aluminium ladder and a couple of battered work benches, above which were pinned a number of ancient 'girlie' photographs. Being a connoisseur of such antiques, and in need of a little cheer, Charlie shuffled over to take a closer look, whilst Lytton disappeared into a small room off the workshop area.

Russell followed, keen to see what he was doing.

'Anything I can do to help, Mr Lytton?'

But before he could reach the office door, Lytton reappeared, carrying two large canvas holdalls, and dumped them at Russell's feet. 'Unpack these,' he said, returning to the room.

Ignoring the command, Russell moved cautiously nearer the office door, but was disturbed by the sudden re-emergence of Lytton with two more bags. 'Griffiths!'

Charlie turned from the art gallery and gazed at the holdalls. Although his spirits had risen slightly, he now felt confused. 'I thought we were doing a diamond job, Mr Lytton.'

'That's right, Griffiths.'

'Then what are we doing here?'

Lytton crossed to the sleepers covering the inspection pit and pushed one aside with his foot. 'It may come as a great disappointment to you, Griffiths, but I do not intend we enter the Diamond Exchange, guns blazing, faces covered with nylon stockings.'

That's good, thought Charlie, as he was allergic to nylon.

'This is how we will enter,' continued Lytton, indicating the pit. 'At the bottom is an abandoned sewer pipe. All we need do is break through its wall and we will have the perfect path to our goal.'

Charlie smiled. He liked the idea. It was simple. Yet one thing still concerned him. 'How do we get at the diamonds?'

'By blowing a hole in the basement wall of the Diamond Exchange. It runs alongside a nearby sewer.'

'You do that and you'll have the old bill down on us!'

Lytton shook his head. 'The vibration will activate every alarm for miles. The police won't know where to

21

look first.'

Now Russell knew the destination of the seven kilos of plastic he had supplied. The 'Man of Mystery', he decided, was fast turning into an old-fashioned villain.

While Russell and Griffiths unpacked boilersuits, boots and hard hats from the canvas holdalls, Lytton returned to the office and closed the door. A moment later a soft, electrical hum was heard. Russell hurried to the door and listened.

'Mr Lytton won't like you prying,' muttered Charlie.

'Can't you hear that noise?'

Charlie didn't look up from unpacking his bag. 'I've found it best not to interfere in Mr Lytton's business.'

Russell considered entering the room and confronting him, but his instinct said it was too soon. Although he now knew Lytton's intention, he still didn't know whether there was anyone else involved, or who Lytton was using to fence the diamonds. To act now would not only blow his over, but without proper back-up could also cost him his life. Lytton was tough, not a man who would accept arrest with quiet equanimity and the muttered cliché: 'It's a fair cop, guv.'

Reluctantly Russell returned to unpacking his holdall. He would wait for Lytton's next move.

2

The Perfect Crime

By the time Joe Payne had returned from parking the car, Russell and Charlie had changed into the overalls and boots.

While Joe scrambled out of his street clothes, Charlie opened the third canvas bag. In it he found rope, a couple of sledge hammers and an assortment of stone-cutting tools. In the fourth bag were empty backpacks, water bottles, a supply of emergency rations and a number of heavy-duty torches.

Playfully, Charlie switched one on and shone it at Joe as he struggled, half hidden in a cloud of cigarette smoke, to pull on a boot. The joke was not appreciated, as the muttered obscenities made clear.

Suddenly the door of the office was thrown open and Lytton emerged carrying a backpack and something wrapped in an old blanket. He too had changed into a black boilersuit and was also wearing a hard hat with a miner's lamp attached. He crossed to one of the benches at the end of the workshop, put down his pack and started to unwrap the blanket.

Russell watched, wondering if there were time to

inspect the office, but paused when the unwrapped bundle produced a machine pistol. 'Bit excessive, just for a few diamonds,' protested Russell.

Lytton didn't answer. Instead he removed a magazine from his backpack and inserted it into the pistol. He then pulled back the bolt and released it with a harsh, metallic clack: the gun was cocked and ready for use.

'You shoot that thing off,' bemoaned Charlie, 'and you'll have old bill calling out the SAS!'

Lytton snapped on the gun's safety catch. 'Armed robbery is armed robbery, Griffiths. The size or power of the gun is unimportant...' He paused as much for dramatic effect, as to let Charlie think about his statement. 'If we're caught, we'll go to prison for a very long time...' He then held up the gun to emphasise the point. '*This* is our insurance against that happening.' Lytton then turned to Payne, who by this time was attempting to hide behind a self-induced smoke-screen. 'And what about you?'

Joe glanced furtively, almost a little ashamedly, at Russell and Griffiths. 'Well...' he said at last, 'I'm with you, Mr Lytton.'

'"I'm with you, Mr Lytton"!' mocked Charlie. 'You mean you're with anyone who pays you.'

'If you're dissatisfied with the arrangement, Griffiths, it isn't too late to back out.'

Charlie eyed Lytton reproachfully. Although he hated guns, he had also acquired a taste for his improved standard of living. 'All right,' he said reluctantly, 'count me in.'

Lytton then turned to Russell. 'And you?'

Russell nodded his acceptance.

But then Lytton knew he would; as an undercover

policeman he had no other choice. So as a special reward, for devotion to duty, he allowed Russell the tedium of breaking through the wall into the sewers.

The tunnel was dark, cold and dank. Somewhere in the gloom, the sound of cascading water could be heard. Like so many of London's sewer tunnels, this was a monument to the skill of the Victorian bricklayer. As a rule, only the brown rat and the occasional workman were ever privileged to view these structures, yet their daily use was shared by the whole population. Once the greatest, now part of the most neglected sewer system in the world, this particular tunnel was to experience further degradation as Russell's sledgehammer sent a scurry of bricks tumbling from the roof.

Slowly the incipient hole was widened until it was large enough for a man to pass through. When this was finished, an aluminium ladder was lowered and Griffiths, also carrying a sledgehammer, and followed by the others, descended into the tunnel. Once they were safely down, Lytton consulted a map, then indicated the direction they should take. With Charlie grumbling about the tightness of his boots, the trio moved off.

In another part of the sewer stood a large metallic shape. At first glance, it looked like a huge black suit of medieval plate armour. Yet the incongruity of the sight would soon be overshadowed by the unnerving realisation that the rasping noise, emanating from a box mounted on the chest-plate, was, in fact, the sound of breathing.

Suddenly the shape gave a small jerky movement as though irritated by something. Then its massive head slowly turned, responding to the distant noise of human activity.

After a moment's intense monitoring, the metal shape moved off along the tunnel, towards the source of the sound.

Despite the ease of Lytton's route, his team were beginning to tire. What was more, Charlie's earlier whinging was now justified as he had developed a nasty case of blistered heels. As he struggled to remove his boots, Joe, who was now dying for a smoke, irritably pulled the first-aid kit from his pack, and while Charlie attended to his injury the others tried to rest as best they could in the unpleasant conditions. The tunnel was damp and smelly, and because of the wet floor, they were forced to perch uncomfortably on their packs.

No one spoke.

No one wanted to.

Yet something else was now agitating Joe. Quietly he crossed to where Lytton was sitting and squatted down beside him. 'It could be my imagination,' he whispered, pointing back along the tunnel, 'but I think there's someone out there.'

Lytton unfastened a pocket flap and produced a Beretta 92. 'Perhaps you should take a look,' he said, offering the gun to Joe. Without comment Joe took the gun, crossed to his pack and slipped it on. Watched by Russell and Griffiths, he then made his way back along the dank tunnel. 'Come on,' said Lytton, 'we have a lot to do. Payne can catch us up later.'

Reluctantly, Charlie scrambled to his feet, his concern growing at the sight of yet another gun. Things were turning very sour, he thought. Sadly he picked up his pack and limped into the gloom after the others.

Payne rounded a corner and entered the adjacent tunnel.
Silently he eased himself into a small alcove, turned out
his helmet-lamp and rummaged in a pocket for a packet
of cigarettes. A moment later there was a hiss of butane,
the rasp of flint against steel, followed by a contented
sigh as Joe inhaled the tobacco smoke. Having to lie to
Lytton about hearing someone following had been worth
it, he thought, puffing hard on the cigarette.

Such was his contentment, he didn't hear the clunk of
metal against brickwork or the rasping sound of a
respirator. When he finally did, he thought it was Lytton
and he started to panic.

Tearing the cigarette and a layer of skin from his dry
lips, he threw the thing into the gloom, as he nervously
tried to ease himself deeper into the alcove. In his
confusion, he hadn't noticed that the clunking had
stopped. Neither had he considered that there *really*
might be someone stalking them. When he finally did, it
was too late.

Suddenly a massive black arm shot into the alcove,
lifting him from the ground and effortlessly hurling him
across the tunnel. Joe hit the wall with a sickening thud,
and could do little more than slither down it like dirty
water.

Quickly his attacker moved in for the kill. Raising his
arm, there was a loud terrifying swish as he brought it
down across the back of Joe's neck, smashing his spinal
cord.

Without pausing, and leaving the dead man where he
lay, the black shape, respirator rasping, moved off in the
direction of the remaining members of Lytton's team.

*

27

Oblivious of what had occurred, Russell and Charlie were examining an unexpected brickwall blocking the tunnel.

'That will have to come down,' said Lytton, studying his map.

Griffiths fingered the wall. 'Does this lead to the Diamond Exchange?'

Lytton shook his head. 'Which means we can't use the explosives. It would alert the police before we were ready.'

Griffiths scowled. 'We have to take it down by hand?'

'That's right.'

'And how thick is it?'

'Less than you, Griffiths,' came the reply, without a trace of humour.

'That's not very kind, Mr Lytton.'

But then he hadn't meant it to be.

Yet in spite of the banter, something was definitely wrong. Russell noticed a certain nervy tentativeness had developed in Lytton's tone. For some reason, the discovery of the wall had disturbed him, and it annoyed Russell that he didn't know why.

Charlie, of course, hadn't noticed anything. He was far too busy rolling up his sleeves, spitting on his hands and practising other preparatory rituals beloved of those about to engage in hard manual labour. In the trade it is known as 'psyching up', and Charlie displayed enormous acumen in the technique. He also swung an impressive sledge, taking but a few minutes to cut a metre-square hole, three layers of brick deep.

Charlie was enjoying himself. He liked this sort of physical exercise, and such was his technique (a skill acquired during a brief sojourn with the local council), he could happily swing the hammer all day.

Yet in spite of Charlie's impressive progress, Lytton was still agitated. Suddenly he turned and walked away from the wall, ducking the splinters of flying brick. Russell followed. 'Are you all right?'

'It's the noise,' Lytton lied. 'It's making my head ache.' But then he thought of a better excuse. 'I'm also concerned about Payne. He's been gone too long.'

The lie proved plausible. 'I could go and look for him.'

'And stumble over each other in the dark?' Lytton shook his head. 'That way you could finish up killing each other.'

As he spoke, a large, black shape turned into the tunnel some way ahead and started to walk towards them. Russell felt uneasy as though something evil had entered their presence.

'It's Payne,' muttered Lytton.

'You're wrong,' came the reply, as Russell grabbed Lytton's arm and pulled him to a halt. 'Look at the height and bulk of the body – it's far too big!'

Lytton brushed away the restraining hand. 'Nonsense,' he said, and again started to walk towards the creature. As he did, his helmet-light picked out its black face. Where there should have been eyes and a mouth, there were slits. Instead of ears, there were what appeared to be inverted horns that continued parallel with the side of the head, until turning ninety degrees and joining some sort of boss-like device situated at its crown.

Although Russell had caught only a glimpse of the face, he knew that its owner intended them harm. The sense of evil he had felt earlier had not been unjustified. 'Challenge him!' he screamed. 'Better still – kill him!'

But Lytton wasn't listening.

Charlie, who had been disturbed by the shouting, abandoned his hammer and joined Russell. On seeing the creature – and Russell's fear – he experienced an unaccustomed sense of bravado. Quickly he sped down the tunnel towards Lytton and the machine pistol he was clutching. Grabbing the gun, Charlie simultaneously shoulder-butted him to one side and fired, spraying the creature's head with the full contents of the magazine and ripping open tubes along its neck. With green fluid gushing from the fractures, the creature collapsed.

Triumphantly, Charlie threw the empty gun to one side and turned back to Lytton. Only to find more of the creatures, silver this time, but just as menacing. Behind them he could see that a section of the sewer wall, like a huge door, had swung open. Framed in the doorway were yet more silver things. Terrified, Charlie slowly raised his hands as Lytton stepped forward and bowed to one of the creatures.

'We are your prisoners, Leader,' Lytton said, almost sounding pleased by the fact. Charlie was even more confused. 'I'm sorry to disappoint you, Griffiths, but this meeting had always been my true destination.'

Charlie nodded. It all made a bizarre sort of sense. At the back of his mind, in the deepest pit of his subconscious, he knew that robbing the Diamond Exchange had been too good to be true. 'Aren't you gonna introduce me?'

'Of course.' Lytton gave another respectful nod. 'These, Griffiths, are your new masters...'

Charlie stared at the implacable metal faces. 'Oh yeah... And what are they?'

'Cybermen! Undisputed masters of the galaxy!'

Such was Lytton's tone, Charlie half expected a

dramatic drumroll to follow his statement. Instead, he was pushed into the room that had been hidden by the hinged section of the wall. There all he could do was watch helplessly as the heavy door closed behind him.

When he had woken that morning and discovered it was raining, Charlie had felt uneasy. Things for him had never gone well on wet days, especially where crime was concerned. Now he could only hope that he was still asleep and would soon wake up to find his current situation was nothing more than a nasty dream.

But as powerful metal hands pushed him roughly around, he knew it wouldn't happen. The only nightmare of the situation, he quickly realised, was its bleak, hopeless reality.

Charlie was not a happy man . . .

From an adjoining tunnel, where Russell had managed to hide during the confrontation with the Cybermen, he had witnessed Lytton's passive surrender. Disturbed by events, he had stumbled off to fetch help, but had almost walked into a Cyber patrol. He had panicked and rushed blindly into the labyrinth of tunnels.

Now he was lost.

In spite of his training and years of experience as an undercover policeman, he had never felt so utterly helpless and alone. Exhausted, he dropped onto the wet floor of the tunnel and fell into a fitful sleep.

3

The Peripatetic Doctor

The Time Lords of Gallifrey are a rather strange race. Although the caretakers of the Great Matrix, the possessors of all knowledge, they can also be tedious and small-minded, content to squabble and bid for parochial power in much the same way as leaders of less advanced planets.

Because of their extraordinary power and intimate knowledge of time, the Gallifreyans had espoused a doctrine of non-interference in the political or cultural activities of other planets. But it hadn't lasted. The High Council, the most supreme body of the Time Lords, had been caught with their fingers covered in political intrigue once too often. Even their own propaganda department had lost faith in its ability to lie convincingly.

It was because of this hypocrisy, and an overall general dissatisfaction, fuelled by an itinerant nature, that one of their number stole a Type 40 TARDIS and decided to explore and learn about the Universe for himself.

Although the thief had a name, he decided, as with his planet, to leave all memory of it behind. Rather than assume a new identity, he would simply be known as the

Doctor. Unfortunately the one thing he couldn't abandon was the instability of regeneration, the event which is both a blessing and a scourge of his people.

When a Time Lord is in danger of dying, or his body grown too old to go on working properly, he is able to change his physical shape. This is brought about by a massive release of a hormone known as 'lindos' which first causes the cells to renew, then realign themselves. Although much work had been done by genetic engineers, the process in some cases remained a random one.

Some Time Lords are able to process through their allotted twelve regenerations with enormous grace and dignity, growing older and more handsome with each change. Others leap about to a startling degree, finishing one regeneration a wise, noble elder, only to start the next a youthful, boastful braggart. This, needless to say, can cause enormous emotional and psychological upset; the Doctor, alas, was not exempt from these strains.

Having recently regenerated, he had remained decidedly odd. Whether this was part of his new personality, or a toxic residue from the act itself, Peri, the Doctor's American companion, couldn't tell. Yet whatever it was, she was very worried, especially as he had decided to undertake extensive maintenance work on the TARDIS.

Not only had many of the roundels which covered the walls of the time machine been dismantled, but also the panelling within which they were housed, causing the exposure of vast areas of electronic equipment. Endless runs of heavy cable and countless strips of printed circuits had been dismantled and were lying about in the corridors like abandoned junk.

For days the Doctor had flitted moth-like from one piece of apparatus to another, probing with a sonic lance, bonding with a crystal transreverser. Peri hoped he knew what he was doing, but until the TARDIS was once more placed under the pressures of time travel, no one could be certain.

While the Doctor had been busy, Peri had spent time catching up on her studies, since it was her intention to finish her degree in biology should she ever return to her university in the United States of America on Earth.

Outside her room Peri could hear the Doctor muttering to himself and the occasional high pitch whine of the sonic lance as he tested a component.

Suddenly there was a small explosion. Peri leapt to her feet and threw open the door of her room. 'What is going on?' she demanded.

A bemused Doctor blinked at the component he was holding, switched off the sonic lance and slipped it into his pocket. 'I'm not certain.'

Peri glanced at the Doctor. 'Explosions don't happen by themselves. What were you trying to do?'

'Something I should have done a very long time ago.' The Doctor smiled broadly, the accident seemingly forgotten. 'Repair the chameleon circuit!' He pointed at a massive bank of microcircuitry in front of him. 'Let me explain...'

Peri scowled. Since the Doctor's regeneration she had often heard him declaim on the particular merits of the circuit, but in such complex terms she never understood its function. The last time she had experienced such a form of over-complicated explanation was when she was dating a first-year engineering student at college. Then she had put his lack of intelligibility down to the the fact that the only language he spoke was jargonese. Later she was to learn that Chuck (for that was his name) when asked about the function of a particular machine would instead explain how it worked. Therefore, to him, an aeroplane was all about the ratio of weight to engine thrust or the complex structure of a turbine blade. A simple answer – 'An aeroplane is a powered machine that can fly' – seemed beyond him.

The Time Lord cleared his throat and gazed down at his American companion. 'Well,' he said, in his best pedagogic voice, 'the TARDIS, when working properly, is capable, not unlike myself, of many amazing things.' He paused only to clear the excessive arrogance from his throat. 'One of its many functions is that it can change shape to blend perfectly with its surrounding environment – hence the term chameleon circuit!'

Although having worked that much out for herself, Peri was grateful for the brevity of the description. Deciding that all men were incapable of explaining simple mechanics, she indicated the chaos in the corridor. 'Are you sure you're up to such complex work?' She prodded a nearby component with the toe of her shoe. 'I mean, you've only recently regenerated.'

'Capable?' His tone had become stern. 'And what makes you think I'm not?'

Determined not to be cowed by his overbearing manner she stared directly into his face. 'Well, to be perfectly honest, you still seem a little unstable.'

With hands held firmly behind his back, the Doctor began to pace up and down. 'Unstable?' he mused, trying to sound like some discriminating lexicographer pondering the meaning of the word. 'Unstable,' he repeated, this time his tone tinged with anger.

'UNSTABLE!' His voice boomed and echoed with hurt resonance. 'This is ME, Peri! At this very moment I am as STABLE as I shall ever be!'

Timidly she backed away. 'Is th-that so?' She stuttered. 'Then you can let me out of the TARDIS right now, because I am not putting up with any more of your tantrums.'

If the Doctor heard her demands he didn't respond. Instead he launched into a new barrage of empty rhetoric. 'You must forget how I used to be! I am a Time Lord, a man of science, of temperament and certainly passion! Surely you understand that?'

She did. But her argument was that she could no longer put up with the shouting and posturing that had become part of his personality.

'Listen, Peri...' The Doctor was now calmer. 'Inside, I am a peaceful person... Perhaps on occasion,' he demurred, 'I can be all noise and bluster.' Gently he took her arm. 'But it is *only* bluster... You've nothing to fear. You're quite safe.' The Doctor looked baleful. 'You will stay?'

Peri thought hard. She didn't want to leave in a moment of anger and spend the rest of her life regretting her decision. Yet if she were to stay, things would have to change. 'All right,' she said at last, 'but there are conditions.'

The Doctor was delighted. 'Anything you say!' Gleefully he grabbed her hands and twirled her around. 'And to cement our new understanding, we shall start by taking a surprise holiday!'

Dizzily Peri watched as he sped off down the corridor towards the console room. 'But we haven't discussed the proviso for my staying.'

'I agree to everything!' he called over his shoulder.

Dodging the electronic clutter, and knowing she was being patronised, a worried Peri followed. Not only was she concerned that little in his attitude would change, but that the last time he had arranged a surprise visit, they had spent a week frozen in the heart of a glacier on the planet Vespod Eight. It was an experience she was not keen to repeat.

As she entered the console room, Peri could see the Time Lord scurrying around setting the navigational co-ordinates. 'Where precisely are we going?'

'To a land of rolling hills and green meadows.'

'Does it have a name?'

The Doctor grinned. 'That's the surprise!'

With the co-ordinates set, he drove his thumb into the master control, but instead of launching the TARDIS safely on its journey, the ship went into a wild spin, the centrifugal force hurling Peri across the room and pinning her to a wall.

'What's happening?' she screamed.

'Stabilisers,' he gasped, desperately trying to maintain his grip on the console. 'I forgot to reset them.'

While Peri, wracked with pain, wondered what *else* he had forgotten, the superstructure of the TARDIS began to creak and groan. If I am to die, she prayed involuntarily, let me be crushed rather than exploded in the vacuum of space.

Pressure increased as the room continued to turn. Gradually, and with enormous effort, the Doctor managed to kick open a small hatch covering the manual override for the stabilisers at the base of the console's pedestal. Watched by Peri, her face now distorted by the G-force, he slowly and painfully worked his way down to the opening. With leaden fingers he pulled at the stabiliser's controls, but nothing happened. Summoning all his strength he tugged again, but still it refused to move. Realising he must generate more leverage, the Doctor knew he would have to exploit the additional force generated by the spinning room. This meant releasing the hold his entwined legs had around the pedestal and allowing his body to swing out like a gondola on a swirling merry-go-round. Yet if his grip failed, it would mean certain death: like Peri, he would be helplessly pinned against the console-room wall.

Aware that there was no other choice, the Doctor carefully locked his fingers around the controls. Satisfied that his grip was the strongest possible, he released his legs.

Pain tore through his arms and shoulders as his body snapped ridged under the G-force, but his grip held. Then slowly, very slowly, the controls began to move, and the stabilisers took effect.

It was a full hour after the room had ceased spinning that the Doctor summoned up both the strength and inclination to move. Slowly he picked himself up, massaged the strained muscles in his shoulders, then crossed to Peri. Dazed, but unharmed, she lay in an undignified heap at the base of the wall against which she had been pinioned. Gently he untangled her but, instead of finding gratitude, he faced a Peri who was spitting with rage and demanding answers about what had happened.

Unable to deny his carelessness, the Doctor could only offer an embarrassed apology. 'At least the TARDIS isn't damaged,' he added in feeble mitigation. He then checked the navigational co-ordinates. 'Neither are we lost.'

Delighted that something had gone right, he operated the scanner-screen. But instead of the expected blue and white beauty of the planet Earth, he was greeted by a white blob.

'And what is *that*?" demanded his irate companion.

The Doctor scratched his head. 'A comet...'

'Is that what we've come to see?'

'Almost...' he lied.

Concerned that his flight computer said they were very close to Earth, but seeing no sign of the planet, the Doctor set to work to locate what had gone wrong.

Frantically he worked on his calculations, his face becoming more grave as the minutes passed. Then suddenly the Time Lord looked up from the computer and smiled broadly. 'Found it!'

'What?'

'You are looking at Comet nine, oblique, one two, oblique, four four.'

Peri glanced at the white blob on the screen and shrugged. 'So?'

'It's Halley's Comet!' he added triumphantly. 'What's more, we are in your solar system in the year calculated as one nine eight five Anno Domini. In other words, you're almost home.'

Peri wasn't so certain. She knew that the white blob on the screen could be *any* comet *anywhere* in the Universe. 'Are you sure that's Halley's Comet?'

'Without doubt.'

'Then where's its tail?'

The Doctor was surprised, not so much by the question, as his companion's ignorance. 'Surely you know that only forms as it nears the Sun?'

She did; and was simply checking to see if the Doctor remembered. After their recent ride in the TARDIS, she was no longer certain about anything the Time Lord said.

'Would you like to take a closer look?'

Peri gazed at the dirty, icy shape and shook her head. Too much had already happened that day. Colliding with Halley's Comet was a treat, she decided, they could save for another occasion.

The time rotor pulsed as the TARDIS hung in space. On the scanner-screen Halley's Comet was still visible.

The Doctor had spent the last few hours checking the propulsion and auxiliary support systems, while Peri had refitted many of the covers to the roundals. If nothing else, the console room looked tidier and more functional. Only time would tell whether the TARDIS itself would pass muster.

Peri watched as the Doctor made final adjustments to the flight computer. 'Soon be ready,' he said, closing the casing around the keyboard. 'Just need to recalibrate the lateral balance cones.'

'Anything I can do?'

'Cross your fingers and hope I've reassembled everything correctly,' he muttered, disappearing into the corridor.

Peri operated the scanner's zoom device and the surface of the comet filled the screen. It was a rough, inhospitable landscape, every inch the frozen, gaseous snowball described by her college lecturer. She flicked a button and the scanner's eye slowly started to pan across the scarred surface. As the lens picked out riffs and long, narrow ditches, a strange, eerie pulse began to emanate from the console. Fearing the worst Peri called the Doctor.

Instantly he popped his head round the door and listened to the sound for a moment before crossing to the console. He increased the volume and continued to listen. 'Sounds like an intergalactic distress call...' He fiddled with some switches, directing the signal through the computer. 'Although the code is certainly unorthodox.'

'Can you decipher it?'

'That doesn't concern me at the moment.' The computer started to punch up data onto the monitor. 'I'm more concerned with tracing its source.'

Indicating it had supplied all available information, the computer let out a tiny bleep. Quickly the Doctor read the screen. Concerned by what he had learned, he re-read it.

'What's the matter?' Peri could see from his expression that something was wrong. 'Have you located the source?'

He nodded as he instructed the computer to recheck the information.

'Well...' insisted Peri. 'Or am I supposed to guess?'

The Doctor scratched his head as the computer reconfirmed the signal's source. 'I don't think you're going to like this...'

His tone confirmed her worst fear. 'It's from Earth, isn't it?'

'I'm afraid so.'

'In *1985*!' Peri was distraught. 'How could space-travellers have got there?'

The Doctor shrugged. 'Others have trapped themselves before,' he said, matter-of-factly, as he locked the automatic navigational guidance system onto the distress call. 'And not all of them were hostile.'

Peri recalled the stories he had told of attempted invasions by Daleks and other alien life forms. 'But what if these *are*?'

The Time Lord smiled. 'One step at a time, Peri. Let's locate them first.'

And before she could argue further, he pressed the master control and the TARDIS followed the beam down to the planet's surface.

4

The Search Begins

It was raining as the time machine materialised on Earth.
What was more, all the Doctor's efforts to reactivate its
chameleon circuit had proved a failure, as the TARDIS
still paraded the outward appearance and livery of an
obsolete British Police telephone box.

The door of the time machine opened and the Doctor
emerged, clutching a tracking device, followed by Peri.
The scene which greeted them was one of waste and
dereliction. It was as though a whirlwind, after a mad
dash through the department stores of the world, had
tired of its hoard and abandoned it, creating an
enormous rubbish tip.

Horrified, Peri gazed at the mess. 'The aliens haven't
done this?' she inquired.

'I shouldn't think so,' he said, scrutinising the dial on
the direction finder. 'We're in a scrap yard somewhere in
London, not a post-holocaust battlefield.'

'Then where are the aliens?'

'Not here,' he said. 'But if my calculations are correct,
we should find them, or at least the source of their signal,
in the next street.'

As the duo walked towards the gates, they heard a terrible grinding and crunching sound. Quickly they turned and saw the last stage of the TARDIS metamorphosing into a pristine Victorian kitchen range.

'Oh neat, Doctor!' Peri laughed. 'Very neat. That doesn't look at all incongruous.'

The Time Lord felt sad. He had spent days working on the chameleon circuit and was certain he had repaired it. 'At least it changed,' he said, defensively.

'Oh, sure. Now it draws even more attention to itself.'

With Peri still chuckling, they passed through the gates of the yard and into the street. Again the Doctor checked his direction finder and pointed the way they should go.

Further up the road, two uniformed policemen stood in the shadow of a large tree. Neither spoke, but then neither needed to, for they knew exactly what each other was thinking. If the Doctor had been less preoccupied, he would have recognised them from his last visit to Earth. He might even have tuned into their telepathic communication. But he didn't and instead walked blindly by. Once he was gone, the policemen, with the carefully measured tread of experienced bobbies, followed.

It had stopped raining and a watery sun was attempting to break through the thinning clouds. Puddles littered the pavements, and the odd passer-by, undecided about the weather, still held high his damp umbrella.

None of this interested the Doctor as he stood before a large boarded-up house, a loud whining from his tracking device announcing they had arrived at the source of the distress signal.

44

Followed by Peri, he climbed the steps to the front door and peered through the letter-box.

'Can you see anything?'

Shaking his head, the Doctor stood up and again checked the tracking device. 'The signal definitely emanates from here,' he said, prodding the front door with an index finger. 'Yet no one appears to live here.'

'It doesn't make sense. Why send out a distress call then not bother to hang around?' Slowly Peri descended the steps, counting each one as she went, '*Unless* they were *forced* to move on.'

Suddenly the Doctor's face lit up. 'Not quite, Peri,' he beamed. 'I don't think they were ever here!'

'But you said the signal came from the house.'

'It does,' he cried, waving the tracking device at her. 'But there is more than one signal!' Without waiting to explain further, the Doctor bounded down the steps and off along the street. 'Come on,' he shouted.

Dutifully, Peri followed, although her high heels were quite unsuited to running. 'Hang on,' she called. 'Anyway, where are we going?'

'Back to the TARDIS!'

Silently, the two policemen watched from a doorway as the pair sped off. Then they turned and began to walk in the opposite direction, knowing where the Doctor would soon arrive.

It had taken some minutes for them to locate the entrance to the newly formed TARDIS. But once inside the console room, the Doctor plugged the tracking device into the computer and switched on. Instantly lights began to flash, sending him into a frantic *pas de deux* with the controls.

Despondently Peri watched this slightly macabre dance until she became fed up. 'Why is it I always have to ask what you're doing?' she declared glumly. 'Why do you never tell me?'

The Time Lord looked up from his work. 'Because I thought it was obvious,' he said.

'Well it isn't! And neither have you told me what you discovered at the house.'

'Deliberate confusion,' he said, triumphantly, as he finished setting the navigational co-ordinates. 'Our alien is being ultra-cautious. He's bouncing his signal off several relay points. The house is simply a focal point to confuse the unwary. What's more it would take current Earth technology days to find where the true signal was coming from.'

Peri was confused. 'Why do that?'

'To buy time, I should think, so that he can confirm if he wants rescuing by the likes of us.'

'Then they must be watching the house. Otherwise how would the alien know the rescuer had arrived?'

'Precisely!'

'So what are you going to do?'

The Doctor unplugged the direction finder from the console. 'Fortunately TARDIS technology is a little better than that of Earth.'

'You've located the true source of the signal?'

The Time Lord nodded as he pressed the master control. 'Should be there almost immediately.'

The time rotor at the centre of the console started to oscillate. 'I hope this alien appreciates what we're doing.'

The Doctor chuckled. 'I'm sure he's sitting there all of a dither, waiting for us to arrive.'

Peri wasn't so certain.

*

A large pipe organ had suddenly appeared on the forecourts of a boarded-up garage. The Doctor hadn't said anything as they squeezed from behind it. He hadn't needed to as his look of disappointment had stated everything on his behalf – the chameleon circuit still wasn't working properly.

Briskly they pulled open the unlocked garage door and were greeted by the sour, pungent smell of sump oil blended with sewer gas.

The Doctor sniffed the air as Peri coughed. 'It's horrible!' she spluttered.

'From the predominant odour of mixed hydro-carbons, it would suggest this area has been used for repairing the internal combustion engine.'

'I think you could be right,' said Peri, eyeing the faded sign above the door. 'But is the alien here? This place looks as deserted as the house.'

The Doctor extended his arm, inviting her to enter. 'Let's find out,' he said.

It took a moment or two for their eyes to adjust to the sepulchral gloom of the workshop and yet another before they noticed the inspection pit surrounded by its debris of soil and bricks.

Cautiously the Doctor crossed to it, picking up a handful of rubble as he went. Tossing it into the pit, he listened as it bounced and ricocheted off the sides of the hole before hitting the floor of the sewer. He then peered over the edge into the darkness.

'Is the alien down there?' whispered Peri, as she joined him.

'Not that I can see,' he said, rummaging in his coat pocket. 'But wherever he is, I'm certain he won't be far from the source of the distress call.'

Producing the tracking device, and after having picked fluff and other substances from its read-out display, the Doctor set the controls and slowly scanned the room. A moment later the machine was alive with information, indicating that the transmitter was in the office at the end of the workshop.

'Wait here,' said the Doctor, as he moved warily towards the room.

Quietly he eased open the door and peered inside. The office was small and stuffy, with a row of metal lockers crowding the length of its longest wall. At the far end of the room was a table with a pair of well-polished shoes on its chipped top. Near the table was a Bauhaus chair – its cane seat destroyed by careless use – with a fashionable grey suit, a crisp white shirt and a silk tie draped neatly over it. Whatever else, thought the Doctor, the alien was a smart if somewhat conservative dresser. It also told him he was humanoid in shape.

Checking there wasn't anyone behind the door, the Doctor entered and switched on the bright, unshaded light. He no longer needed his tracking device to locate the transmitter as the draped suit told him its precise location. From what the Doctor had already seen, he knew that the suit's wearer was far too tidy not to have hung it in a locker, *unless* the lockers were already full of something else.

With careful vigilance, the Doctor inspected the cabinets for signs of booby-traps. Taking out his sonic lance, he ran it across the surface of one of the doors. This, he hoped, would deactivate any sensors primed to set off a detonator. Even so, he knew that there were many other ways to protect a cabinet when the only way in, without specialised tools, was the conventional method of turning the handle and opening the door.

Rubbing his hands along the outside of his thighs, the Doctor wiped the nervous sweat from his palms. It had crossed his mind to wait for the alien to return rather than risk the possibility of instant death. But the Doctor also knew that, should the creature prove hostile, it would be useful to know something about where he came from before encountering him. To learn this, he would have to examine the technology inside the cabinet.

Deciding he must take the risk, the Doctor grabbed the cabinet handle, but the door wouldn't open. Delighted that nothing unpleasant had so far occurred, he found a piece of wire in his pocket and began to probe the lock. As he worked, his concentration was interrupted by a small voice calling from far in the distance. At first he didn't take any notice, but the voice was insistent, and called again. This time the Doctor recognised it as Peri's. When she called yet again, he heard the fear and tension.

Concerned, yet not displeased at having to postpone his current task, he ran back into the workshop and found a scared Peri with hands held high above her head. Standing in the inspection pit, with only the top part of his body showing, was one of the policemen. In his hand was a gun.

It was the sight of this somewhat surreal tableau rather than the awareness of any danger which caused the Doctor to skid to a halt. 'Ah,' he said, his tone somewhat bemused, 'how do you do, Constable.'

The policeman didn't reply, and instead waved his gun, indicating that he should move to where Perio was standing.

Reluctantly the Doctor complied and started to

shuffle towards her. As he neared the pit, he suddenly extended his hand in an offer of help. 'You look so uncomfortable in that hole,' he said, in an exuberant manner. 'Are you sure you wouldn't like me to help you out?'

Such was the speed of his movement, it momentarily confused the policeman, giving the Doctor enough time to trap the barrel of the gun against the floor beneath the sole of his shoe. As he struggled to free it, the Time Lord stamped repeatedly on the policeman's hands with his free foot, causing him to release his grip and to fall into the murky depths of the pit. Before jumping after him, the Doctor kicked the liberated revolver along the floor to Peri, who blocked its slithering motion with her foot.

Although she had been taught to use a gun by her father, she still didn't like handling them. It was the idea such weapons were exclusively designed to kill people that she hated most.

With great reluctance she bent to pick up the gun. As her fingers stretched towards it, she became aware of a movement near the door. Looking up, she saw the second policeman enter the workshop, carrying a large calibre automatic.

Leaving her own gun where it lay, Peri slowly stood up and gave the policeman one of her deliberate, helpless female looks. 'I must sit down,' she said weakly. 'I feel faint.'

Lowering herself onto a pile of soil near the inspection pit, Peri waited for the policeman to reach her. As he neared, she quickly grabbed a handful of soil and threw it into his face. Although he managed to parry most of it with a protective arm across his eyes, the action gave her enough time to scramble across the floor and retrieve her own gun.

As Peri levelled it to his chest, she said, as aggressively as her fear would allow, 'Throw down your gun.'

Instead of obeying, the policeman smiled: in the inspection pit behind her he could see the top of his colleague's helmet.

'I said, throw down your gun!'

Reluctantly the policeman obeyed.

Aware that the pit was behind her, and also who had recently disappeared into it, Peri glanced over her shoulder. Seeing the helmet, she quickly backed towards it, while keeping the gun trained on her prisoner. But instead of the expected second policeman, she found an amused Doctor.

'I see you have everything under control,' he said, clambering out.

'I wished you'd coughed or something.' Peri was furious. 'The sight of that helmet scared me half to death!'

'Sorry about that,' he said, removing it and tossing it to one side. 'Thought it might amuse.'

Peri couldn't agree. Neither could the policeman, as the Time Lord's arrival had turned the impending pleasure of his release into the sour anger of defeat. Neither was his humour improved when the Doctor insisted upon searching him.

Apart from a truncheon and handcuffs, he also found several clips of ammunition, a switchblade knife, a knuckle duster, two hand grenades and a small canister of tear gas.

Relieved the policeman hadn't attempted to use any of these, Peri watched as each article, except the handcuffs, was thrown onto a pile of soil alongside the pit. Finishing his search, the Doctor snapped a cuff onto the policeman's wrist, lead him to a work bench at the end of the room and fastened the other cuff to its leg.

'Key, please,' he demanded.

Reluctantly the constable produced it from its hiding place inside the top of his sock.

Slipping the key into his pocket, the Doctor unclipped the policeman's radio. 'Now . . .' he said, adding it to the pile of other confiscated items, 'what's all this gun-waving business about?'

The policeman remained implacable, staring almost trance-like at nothing in particular.

'Didn't think you'd be very talkative. More frightened of someone else than you are of me, eh?'

There was still no reply.

'I assume he isn't a genuine policeman?' Peri asked.

The Doctor nodded. 'Neither was the one in the pit.'

'Then I think we should fetch some *real* ones,' she insisted, edging towards the door, 'and right now!'

Oh, no! thought the Doctor. Things were far too delicate to involve them. 'In a while, Peri. At least not before I've made a few inquiries of my own.'

Peri had met this sort of prevarication before. Usually she would accept his dashing off, but this was twentieth-century Earth. Here he didn't need to become involved. Here he could allow the proper authorities to sort things out. 'But it isn't necessary to make inquiries,' she said, firmly. 'We have our own very efficient police –'

'Who, I suppose –' his tone was more sarcastic than intended – 'have enormous experience in tracking down and dealing with stranded alien life-forms?'

She couldn't reply, her argument having seized up like

52

a moving engine suddenly drained of oil.

'Involving the police will not help,' he continued. 'At least not at the moment.'

'Maybe you have a point. But there's no need to do everything your self. Especially after your recent regeneration.'

'Look, Peri, I won't deny that I am a little confused, but I am in control of my faculties most of the time.' He crossed to the inspection pit and looked into it. 'What's more, I have a horrible feeling that we are now dealing with more than a stranded Alien.'

'Oh ...' She suddenly felt uneasy. 'What makes you think that?'

Pointing at the policeman, the Doctor said: 'Because of him and his colleague in the sewer. I've met them before. I think it was the last time I was on Earth.'

'Who were they with?'

'That's the trouble, I can't remember.' The Doctor pressed his temples with the tips of his fingers as though trying to wring the information from his mind. 'My memory's still scrambled from the effects of my regeneration.'

'Are you sure you shouldn't involve the police?' Peri eyed the impostor cuffed to the table and added in low voice, 'If the Alien is using armed men like him, he can't be that friendly.'

The Doctor nodded. 'Look, I'll make a deal with you,' he said. 'Give me an hour to make my own inquiries, and then you can go to the police.'

She knew where his 'inquiries' would take him, and was afraid. 'Does that mean you're going down there into the sewers?' she said, pointing into the pit.

Boyishly, the Doctor grinned. 'It's the only place I'll

find the alien.'

Peri edged towards the pit and gazed into the black void. In her imagination she was convinced she could hear the distant screams of a million souls in torment. *And the Innocents, in search of the truth, descended into the fiery pit of Hell, but all they found was their own eternal damnation.* She couldn't recall where she had first heard those words, and wished her memory had been less efficient at recalling them. What was more, the smell of the sewers had grown stronger, as though eagerly awaiting her impending doom. 'All right...' she said, trying to sound jolly, 'let's get started.'

Taken aback by her abrupt eagerness, the Doctor was overwhelmed. 'You don't have to come if you don't want to. I mean, it could be dangerous.'

'Isn't it always?' she shrugged. 'Anyway, someone has to make sure you return after the agreed hour.'

The Doctor clapped his hands and vigorously rubbed them together like a manic miser. 'Let's get started,' he said. 'I'm pleased you want to come. You'll be very useful.'

Peri couldn't imagine the kind of assistance he expected, as her nerve had gone, and the thought of entering the sewers terrified her. Neither could she believe that the Doctor hadn't seen how afraid she was, and ordered her back to the safety of the TARDIS, as he usually did.

Scared and unhappy, Peri followed the Time Lord as he scrambled into the pit.

After handcuffing the unconscious second policeman to the bottom of the ladder, the Doctor produced a small torch and started to examine the brickwork for recent scuffs and scratches. Satisfying himself he had found the alien's trail, he stalked off into the gloom, stopping from time to time, in the tradition of a Cheyenne or Apache scout, to confirm they were still heading in the right direction. Why he seemed so confident, given that one set of scuff marks looked much like another, Peri would never know. It wasn't that he had established any proven skill in tracking – in fact, quite the reverse. On many occasions Peri had seen him totally lost almost within sight of the TARDIS.

Neither was she happy about having brought along the policeman's gun. Knowing she would never use it, but hoping it would provide a little moral support, she now feared its accidental discharge. Apart from anything else, the gun was heavy, cold to the touch and awkward to carry. 'You wouldn't think this was my first visit to London,' she said, sadly, avoiding a puddle of something very nasty. 'If only I could be allowed to see it like a regular tourist.'

'This route will prove more memorable,' the Doctor said, as he placed his ear to the wet ground.

She sniffed the foul air. 'It makes me feel like Harry Lime... And look what happened to him!'

Unable to hear anything useful, the Doctor scrambled to his feet and stalked off along the tunnel, briefly wondering who Harry Lime was.

Suddenly his eye was attracted by a large collection of scuff marks and he bent to examine them. 'I think we're following more than one person,' he said, excitedly.

'More than one alien?'

'Difficult to tell.' The Doctor stood up. 'But certainly more than one pair of feet have recently passed this way.'

'Then we *must* get help,' Peri insisted.

But before the Time Lord could answer, the sound of a machine pistol firing echoed and rumbled around the sewers.

Afraid, Peri lifted her own gun and waved it about as though looking for someone to point at, but there was only the Doctor, and he was now running in the direction of the gun fire.

'Come on, Peri!' his voice boomed. 'You may get the chance to use that thing. Someone needs our help!'

Peri watched the torch's bright beam dance away along the roof of the tunnel. 'But I don't want to use it!' she screamed. 'I wanna be a regular tourist and visit Buckingham Palace, see Trafalgar Square, and spend hours queuing up outside Madam Tussaud's to see a lot of waxworks I'm not interested in. Don't you understand?'

But the Doctor was gone. And if Peri wished to avoid stumbling around lost in the dark, she would have to catch him up.

And soon.

5

A Close Encounter of a Very Nasty Kind

Payne's body stretched across the width of the tunnel, his head lolling at an extreme and unnatural angle, his face frozen in an expression of perpetual agony. Next to him was the Beretta and the unsmoked cigarette he had abandoned in his moment of panic. In life, Joe had been a hard, unsympathetic man whom few people liked. But now, not even his worst enemy would have taken pleasure in seeing his crumpled corpse strewn across the wet brickwork.

Suddenly the far end of the tunnel was illuminated by the small, searching beam of the Doctor's torch. Quickly it darted from side to side as it scanned the floor ahead of him. A moment later it settled, like a large, tropical butterfly on Joe's anguished face.

The Doctor stared down at the body, as though paying silent respect, before bending to confirm the lack of pulse. He then examined the neck and noticed the massive contusion.

As he pondered on what might have delivered such a blow, a breathless Peri stumbled along the sewer and joined him. It took but a moment to both regain her breath and then realise that the ragdoll shape splayed before her would never move again.

'His neck's been broken,' said the Doctor, quietly.

'Broken?' Peri was confused. 'Then what was that shooting we heard?'

'I don't know yet.'

Seeing the abandoned Beretta, the Time Lord picked it up and smelt the muzzle. 'Hasn't been fired,' he said, flicking on the safety-catch. 'What's more, I've witnessed this method of killing before.'

'Oh... where?'

The Doctor first scratched, then shook his head. 'Wish I could remember. But further investigation might jog my memory.'

Peri wasn't so certain. 'I know I agreed to you searching for an hour,' she said, indicating Payne's body, 'but to me that looks like murder!'

'There still isn't anything the police can do. Not until we find some hard evidence.'

'What more do you need than a body?' There was an incipient note of hysteria in her voice.

'That is the unfortunate victim – we require the perpetrator.'

Slipping the Beretta into his coat pocket, he strode off along the tunnel. 'Come along,' he said, briskly. 'When we've found who is responsible for this murder, *then* you can involve the police!'

The Cybermen's base was a crude affair. The mouth of large sewer pipe had been roughly bricked up, while the other end had been fashioned to house a door. Scattered around the makeshift room, which dripped viscous globules of water, were several large machines with

Cybermen busily working at their controls. Along one side of the tunnel were a number of glass-fronted cabinets, each the size of a telephone box and stuffed full of wires, tubing and electronic probes.

Inside one of the cases was a man suspended from steel ropes. Connected to his head was a shiny, silver skull-cap with a myriad of tiny wires fanning out from its crown and connecting to probes attached to the roof of the cabinet. Covering his arms and legs was another shiny substance, which at first glance looked like aluminium foil. Closer inspection would have shown it to be *arnickleton*: a tough alloy made from metals not found on Earth, and which didn't just cover limbs but actually replaced them. This process would continue until the man's whole body, except his reprocessed brain, had been substituted with the alloy. The procedure was known as Cybernisation: the transformation from human to Cyberman.

At first glance, the almost utilitarian appearance of Cybermen makes them look the same, suggesting a strong egalitarian society. This is far from the case; their hierarchy is rigid. At the apex, and in total command, is the Cyber Controller. Next are Senior Leaders, like a Brigadier on Earth, who command a brigade or, as the Cybermen call it, a Major Phalanx. They are assisted by Leaders and Junior Leaders. Below them is the army, the very heart of the Cyber race, dedicated to absolute supremacy and domination of their galaxy through war and destruction.

Charlie Griffiths watched two such Cybermen in deep conversation and prayed that they weren't discussing his future – or, more importantly, the impending lack of it. Although he couldn't hear what they were saying, their general demeanour suggested they were agitated.

'Impossible!' snapped Lytton, dismissively when Charlie had pointed this out. 'Cybermen do not have emotions, therefore cannot become as you suggest.'

'No emotions?' Charlie was incredulous. 'That isn't possible.'

'Not for them, Griffiths.'

Charlie had never considered himself, other than in the pejorative sense, a passionate man. Yet to live without feeling or emotion seemed to him to be life without purpose. Little things like walking in the park, eating one of his Ma's breakfasts; stroking his cat and listening to her purr; a pint at his local with his mates; or snuggling under his duvet when it was cold outside – all trivial, even silly things, but activities which gave colour and texture to being alive.

Charlie wondered why such creatures continued living, but his consideration was interrupted by the cessation of the 'agitated' Cyberman's conversation.

'You . . .' said one of them, in a flat, mechanical voice, 'will answer my questions.' He strode across to Lytton and prodded him in the chest with the huge metal index and third finger of his left hand. 'How did you know we were here?'

Lytton gave a small bow of respect. 'You have a ship on the dark side of the moon, Leader. I tracked your transmission.'

The Cyber leader turned to his Lieutenant. 'Inform Moon Base at once,' he said flatly, and without any obvious sense of concern or urgency. 'Our signals have been detected. We must increase distortion –'

'You're quite safe, Leader,' interrupted Lytton.

'Earth authorities are unable to receive your transmissions.'

'You did,' said the Leader.

'But I am not from Earth...'

Charlie glanced at Lytton. He didn't like the sound of his mendacious bluff – at least he hoped it was a bluff...

'I am from Vita Fifteen,' Lytton continued almost casually, 'in the star system six-nine-zero. My planet is known as Riften Five.'

'I have heard of that place.' The Leader menacingly placed his metal face very close to Lytton's. 'It is inhabited by a race of warriors called Charnels, who fight only for money.'

Lytton, as surreptitiously as the situation would allow, attempted to pull away from the Cyberman. 'I am here to aid you in your cause,' he said, with less confidence than before. 'If I'd wished to betray you, I would have informed Earth Authorities, not risked my life coming here.'

There was a moment's deathly silence as the Cyber Leader considered what had been said. 'There is logic in your statement,' he uttered.

Lytton gave another little bow. 'Thank you, Leader.'

'I shall inform the Cyber Controller of your capture. He will decide your fate.'

Lytton glanced eagerly around the room. 'Is he here?'

'If you have been monitoring our transmission, you will know where he is.'

'Then he must still be on Telos?'

The Cyber Leader nodded. 'You and your companion,' he said, indicating Charlie, 'will be taken to him.'

Charlie Griffiths wasn't certain what to make of the conversation he had just witnessed. He had never heard of Telos, and although it sounded like a Greek island, he found it difficult to believe that there was anywhere inhabited by tall, bulky men with expressionless voices and a fetish for wearing suits made from aluminium foil.

'Tell me this is all a terrible dream, Mr Lytton.'

'Try leaving this room without their permission.'

Charlie looked at the huge robotic, silver shapes and decided he would remain where he was for the time being. 'Where is Telos?'

'Tremulus Three.'

The information didn't help. 'Where's that near, Mr Lytton?'

'Tasker's Crown...'

Somewhere in the confused jumble of Charlie's mind, the name meant something. Perhaps, he thought, it was a pub where he had once been a regular? 'And what about the other stuff you told them. How did you know what to say?' No answer. 'Come on, Mr Lytton – you're not being fair. I mean you even told them you weren't from Earth.'

'Perhaps it's true,' he said at last.

'That's not possible! Anyway, you said you came from north London.'

Lytton let out a slow, deliberate sigh. After two years trapped on Earth he still couldn't believe how stupid some of its inhabitants could be. 'You know, Griffiths, when I talk to someone like you, I wonder why your ancestors bothered to climb out of the primordial slime.'

Given how confused and scared he felt, Charlie was rather inclined to agree.

*

On hands and knees, the Doctor scrutinised a small indentation in a brick at the base of a tunnel wall. However hard he tried to interpret the mark, it delivered the same shrill message. He was utterly and totally lost. Uncertain whether to backtrack or go blindly on in the hope they might accidentally stumble across their quarry, the Doctor stood up. Like his inspiration, his torch was begining to fade. Without light they couldn't stay in the sewers, but neither did he want to pause in his search at such a negative moment.

'Was the man we discovered killed by the alien?'

The Doctor didn't know, and said so.

'But if the alien did do it,' Peri speculated, 'how do you think he'll respond to us?'

'With enormous gratitude I should think. After all, we do have the means of getting him off the planet.'

Peri wasn't so certain. 'And if he doesn't believe you?'

'Then I shall beat him into submission with my charm.'

Although the Doctor's response had been flippant, Peri's concern had rekindled the Time Lord's urgency to find the Alien before it did anything else. Fading batteries or not, they would have to go on.

Slithering over wet bricks, they continued their journey. Ahead they could see a four-way junction, its transverse tunnels directed at the cardinal points of the compass. The Doctor swept the beam of his torch across the floor, searching desperately for a trail, but the dark, shiny surface was unmarked. He checked the walls, but they proved equally pristine.

Reaching the junction they stopped. The Doctor shone his torch into the west tunnel, but it was empty. Then directed his beam northwards and it was swallowed whole by the gloom. As he turned to the east tunnel he heard a faint noise, like that of a boot scuffing against brick. Peri had also heard it and taken out her gun.

'What now?' she whispered.

Placing a finger to his lips, the Doctor switched off his torch and, keeping close to the wall, entered the tunnel where he edged his way cautiously.

Suddenly there was a tug on his sleeve; it was an angry Peri. 'You've no idea what's in here!' she said, furiously. 'It might prove useful to have a plan in case whatever it is turns out to be hostile.'

He knew she was right and it annoyed him that he needed to be reminded of the obvious. 'All right,' he muttered, 'back to the main tunnel.'

As they started to retrace their steps, an arm lurched out of the gloom, wrapped itself around the Time Lord's neck and dragged him out of sight into an alcove. Peri cocked her revolver and shouted: 'I'm armed! Give yourself up!'

A moment later the Doctor was pushed back into view, this time with a human holding a knife to his neck.

'Put the gun down,' the man growled, 'otherwise I'll open up his throat.'

Reluctantly Peri did as she was told.

Pressing the knife even harder against the Doctor's neck, the man frisked him and found the Beretta. 'Over there,' he ordered, pushing the Time Lord towards the wall. 'Both of you!' As the duo obeyed the man picked up Peri's gun and thrust it into his pocket. 'Now hands on the wall and spread your legs!' Again they complied. Removing the Beretta's safety catch, he placed its muzzle at the back of Peri's neck and quickly searched her.

'Who are you?' she inquired nervously when he had finished.

'Police – Detective Sergeant Russell.'

Peri didn't believe him. 'Do you have a badge or something?'

'Undercover policemen don't carry identification.'

The Doctor lowered his hand and half turned to face Russell. 'Then it seems we'll have to take each other on trust.'

'Hands back on the wall!' He did as commanded. 'Now,' said Russell, 'enough of who I am: what are your names?'

The Time Lord cleared his throat, knowing there would be trouble about not being able to provide one. 'Shall if suffice to say that this is Peri and I am known as the Doctor?'

'Doctor who?'

'Actually, it's more a matter of *what*,' he said cautiously. 'I'm a doctor of medicine, science, philosophy –'

'Are you trying to make a fool of me?' the policeman shouted. 'I WANT YOUR NAME!'

The situation was getting silly. And when guns were involved, Peri knew they would soon become dangerous.

'It's unpronounceable,' she said quietly, 'that's why he calls himself the Doctor.'

But Russell wasn't interested in her excuses. 'I'm asking for the last name . . .' he levelled the Beretta. 'WHAT IS YOUR NAME?'

It was at that moment he noticed he was holding the same make of gun Lytton had given to Payne. Whereas he knew there were many Beretta 92s in the world, they were not common enough for the coincidental presence of two in the same London sewer – not even, thought Russell, on a day as bizarre as this. 'Where did you get this?'

Surprised by the sudden change of tack, the Time Lord glanced over his shoulder. 'Er, we found it nearby,' he said.

Russell cocked the gun and pressed it into the small of his back. 'The last time I saw this, it wasn't lost.'

The Doctor grimaced as the muzzle bit into his skin even through his thick coat. 'Well, to be honest,' he said, nervously, 'as the owner was dead, I felt he didn't have any further use for it.'

'Did you kill him?'

He was incredulous. 'For his *gun*?'

'Don't get smart.' Russell's tone was almost vicious. 'I don't like murderers.'

'We found him dead!' insisted Peri.

'I don't believe you.'

Grabbing the back of the Time Lord's collar, he pressed the gun even harder into his spine. 'Now tell me the truth!'

But this was the chance the Doctor had been waiting for. Quickly he jerked his body in a quarter turn, knocking the gun clear of his back, while simultaneously back-kicking Russell's knee. As pain tore through his leg, the policeman released his grip on the Doctor's collar and collapsed.

'Sorry about that,' said the Doctor, crouching to the agonised heap that was Russell, 'but we weren't getting very far with me playing pat-a-cake with the wall.'

'Who are you?' groaned Russell.

'I've already told you: I'm the Doctor. I'm also a Time Lord from the planet Gallifrey.'

'A *Time Lord*?' he repeated, incredulously, wondering how a damaged leg could affect his hearing. 'From another planet?'

The Doctor nodded.

'Then one of us is bonkers!'

That was debatable, he thought. 'But I'm telling the truth.' He stood up and offered a helping hand to Russell. 'The thing is,' he continued, 'are you?'

Grasping the hand, Russell slowly pulled himself to his feet. 'Yes,' he said, 'I am a policeman.'

Peri still wasn't convinced. 'If you are,' she said 'what are you doing down here?'

He smiled: it was a good question, especially as he had been unable to make any sense of the last couple of hours. Russell recalled how conventionally the day had begun. A simple robbery had been planned, yet instead of diamonds he had found huge men dressed in silver suits wandering around the sewers. He had seen Griffiths shoot one of them to pieces, yet no one had cared. Even more curious was that Lytton had known who the silver men were. Although Russell had found the Doctor's story a bizarre invention, he had decided, on reflection, his own hardly sounded any more credible. On the other hand, he considered, there was little to lose by telling them what had occurred. It would prove a useful practice before facing his superiors at Scotland Yard.

Carefully Russell hobbled to the sewer wall and propped himself against it. 'What would you like to know first?' he said, once he was settled.

'Do you know anyone who changed from a grey suit, black shoes, a white shirt and silk tie before entering the sewers?'

He had expected an unusual question but not one as

odd as this. 'Well . . .' he stammered, 'as a matter of fact I do. It was Mr Lytton.'

'Lytton?' the Docor repeated, rolling the word around his mouth as though it were a hard sweet. 'Would that be Gustave Lytton?'

Russell shrugged. 'We've always called him Mr Lytton. He was –'

'Wait a minute,' interrupted Peri, 'how did you know his first name was Gustave?'

The Doctor pondered for a moment. 'I don't know,' he said. 'The Gustave seemed to fit the Lytton quite neatly.'

'Do you know who Gustave Lytton is?'

The Time Lord shook his head.

'Think,' she insisted. 'Somewhere you have information about this man.'

'So what? He may have nothing to do with this.'

'That hardly matters. Word-association has tripped something in your mind. This could be the catalyst you need to unlock your scrambled memory.'

He knew what Peri suggested was true, but was annoyed at her choice of time and place for such an experiment.

'Concentrate!' she demanded. 'Concentrate hard!'

Fury stormed into the Doctor's mind as her insistent voice bored into his brain. Such was his unreasoned frenzy that he momentarily blacked out. When he finally regained control of his senses, he could see, in his mind's eye, the image of a man.

'Wait a moment,' he said, turning to Russell. 'Is Lytton tall, fit, tough –' The Doctor paused for a moment before burbling; 'The sort of man who might shoot his mother just to keep his trigger-finger supple.'

'Well...' the policeman flustered. 'A somewhat colourful description – but it could be him.'

Peri was delighted. 'It worked!' she exclaimed. 'You now know who Lytton is?'

The Doctor nodded. The foggy confusion shrouding areas of his memory had gone. Suddenly everything was clear – and he was not happy.

'I know him,' he remonstrated with himself, 'because I was responsible for his being standed on Earth. No wonder I had a memory block. Anyone would after committing such folly.'

'Who is he?' she asked.

'Commander Gustave Lytton, late of the Dalek Task Force. He is an evil mercenary who will do anything for money – especially if it involves killing.' He angrily punched the palm of his hand. 'I should have known the moment we met those phony uniformed policemen.'

Russell, now completely bewildered, gave an exaggerated cough, more to draw attention to himself than to clear his throat. 'What are you two talking about?' he said.

The Doctor turned to him. 'Like me, Lytton is from another planet. He was stranded here, along with his two bodyguards a couple of years ago...' He paused, an obvious question having occurred to him. 'You did *know* he was an alien?'

Abashed, Russell shook his head.

'Why ever not?'

In utter frustration the policeman threw his hands into the air. 'Because visitors from other planets do not exist!'

'They do,' said Peri. 'I know it's difficult to accept, but there are tens of thousands of inhabited planets in the

Universe.'

'Maybe.' He was becoming defensive. 'But they have yet to travel here.'

Irritated by such stubbornness, the Doctor started to pace up and down. 'If you won't accept what you're being told,' he said, 'at least tell me why you were investigating Lytton.'

Although the question was simple, Russell found it difficult to know where to begin. 'Well...' he said, awkwardly, 'Lytton was a thief. He'd stolen top-secret electronic equipment.'

The Doctor ceased pacing and jabbed an index finger into Russell's chest. 'And I can show you where that equipment is,' he said. 'What's more, it produced the signal that brought us here.'

Russell's mind was in a whirl and didn't know what to believe. It wasn't that the Doctor had produced any hard evidence to support his outrageous statements, but there was a simple, spontaneous honesty about him that made it difficult for the policeman to be entirely dismissive. What was more, he couldn't forget the silver men he had seen, and that the one destroyed by Charlie Griffiths had bled green blood. 'All right...' he said. 'Where is the equipment?'

'In the office of the garage where I found the suit.'

It made sense, thought Russell. He'd heard an electrical hum from the room himself. 'Let's take a look.'

'Before we do, answer me one question: why haven't you arrested Lytton?'

Russell rubbed his sore leg and remembered how disturbed his departmental Chief Superintendent had been – a man not noted for a low panic threshold – when unable to acquire any background information on

Lytton.

'We weren't ready,' the policeman said. 'We needed further information . . . answers to certain questions.'

'Like where he had come from? Why you couldn't trace his birth certificate, or any other expected documentation?' Russell was stunned. 'Well?' insisted the Doctor.

He shrugged. 'Maybe.'

'*Was it as though Lytton had come from another planet?*' he urged, ramming home the truth. The Doctor flicked on the safety-catch of the Beretta and tossed it to a bewildered Russell. 'Come along,' he said, striding off along the tunnel. 'We've wasted enough time here.'

'Where are we going?' Peri inquired, running to catch him up.

'Back to the TARDIS for a rethink.'

The Doctor switched on his torch and pointed it ahead of them.

'Wait!' cried Russell. The duo stopped and turned. 'Can I come with you?'

The Doctor nodded and the policeman hobbled towards them.

As Peri returned to assist him, a tiny lens, mounted in the ceiling of the tunnel recorded their presence . . .

At the Cyberman base the Leader said to Lytton: 'There are three humanoid intruders in the tunnel. Do you know who they are?'

Lytton shook his head.

'P'raps it's the old bill,' muttered Charlie. 'They'll soon sort this fancy-dress party.'

Not understanding Charlie's slang, the Leader demanded a translation from Lytton.

71

'He implies it could be the police.'

'Then they must be dealt with.' The Leader turned to his Lieutenant. 'This time,' he added, indicating the glass cabinets, 'they must not be damaged. We cannot afford to be wasteful. Our forces must grow in strength.'

Lytton gave a tiny smile. Although Charlie witnessed this unique event, he assumed, as he had only ever seen Lytton scowl, that it had been caused by wind. But Charlie was wrong. Lytton was feeling very pleased with himself indeed.

'All these tunnels look the same,' Peri said.

'*This* is the right way,' said the Doctor.

Peri was doubtful. Russell, whose knee had improved, shuffled along dreaming of hot coffee, a rare steak served with sautée potatoes and apple crumble covered in cream. Such was his hunger, he would have been content to eat them all together from the same plate.

Suddenly the Doctor dropped to the floor and started to scrabble about looking for scuffs and scratches.

Peri stooped down next to him. 'We *are* lost.'

'Of course we're not,' he snapped.

Russell, not having the energy to restart if he stopped moving, hobbled past the duo and continued on into the gloom.

'Do *you* know the way?' called Peri.

'I think so,' mumbled the policeman.

The Doctor jumped to his feet as Russell turned into a side tunnel. 'That was the direction I intended to take,' he said tartly, running after him.

Peri followed, ruminating on the churlishness of a jealous Time Lord.

But when they caught up with Russell, they found him

pressed flat against the wall at a point where two tunnels crossed. 'Stop!' he whispered, hoarsely.

They obeyed.

'What is it?' murmured the Doctor.

'Look for yourself.'

Cautiously, he peered into the adjacent tunnel. At the far end he could see, in silhouette, the unmistakable shape of a Cyberman. Like a motionless sentinel, the creature stood tall and erect, its massive form blocking the tunnel. Then suddenly, as though aroused, it jerked into life and started to stride in his direction.

Quickly the Doctor withdrew his head, hoping he hadn't been seen.

'What is it?' asked Peri.

'A Cyberman! A particularly unpleasant life form.' He felt in his pocket for the sonic lance.

'What's it doing here?'

The Doctor scowled. 'That's what I intend to find out.'

He switched on the lance and fiddled with the controls. As he worked, he felt a finger gently prod him in the back. The Doctor turned and saw the butt of the Beretta being proffered by Russell.

The Time Lord smiled. 'Thanks, but no thanks,' he said, holding up the lance. 'This will work even better.'

Peri was horrified. 'You're not going to fight it?' she exclaimed.

He shook his head. 'Just shake it up a little.'

Quickly he glanced into the adjacent tunnel and saw the Cyberman advancing steadily. Holding the sonic lance like a dagger, the Doctor braced himself. As the Cyberman came level with where he was hiding, the Time Lord shot out his arm and thrust the lance into his

73

chest unit.

The effect was immediate. For a moment, the Cyberman froze, statue-like, as though he had been drained of all energy. Then, very slowly, movement returned and he began to stagger and wobble like a drunken man.

The instability worsened, and although the creature clawed at the tunnel's brickwork for support, he couldn't control the wild spasms in his limbs. Then suddenly he let out a terrible roar and started to flail at the air. Smoke began to pour from his respirator as tiny tongues of flame licked and danced along the pipework on his chest. Twisting and turning frantically, as though wrestling some enormous invisible serpent, the Cyberman let out a final terrible, ear-piercing scream and collapsed. A moment later he exploded.

Once the smoke had cleared, the Doctor, followed by Peri and Russell edged their way into the debris-strewn tunnel.

'That was awful!' Peri protested. 'Why did you have to kill him in such a terrible way?'

The Doctor looked fraught. 'I only meant to stun him,' he said, picking up the Cyberman's gun. 'I must have set the lance too high.'

Peri felt sick. 'Can we get away from here?'

The Doctor nodded.

Balancing precariously on his one good leg, Russell had somehow managed to manoeuvre himself into a crouching position. 'It's a robot!' he exclaimed, prodding at a piece of fractured body-plate.

'Not quite.' The Doctor pointed at the oozing head. 'It also had a living brain.'

This observation did not help Peri's stomach.

'What's more, there are bound to be other Cybermen around. We must get away from here and back to the TARDIS.'

The Doctor helped Russell into a standing position.

'How will you deal with them?' asked Peri.

'Surely we'll need the army for that?' chipped in Russell.

The Doctor shook his head. 'These are no ordinary warriors,' he said. 'First we'll need a plan.'

A tiny blue light flashed on the console indicating a Cyberman had been terminated. This event generated concentrated activity in Cyber base. Knowing they had been discovered, the Cybermen's contingency plan had come into operation and they were preparing to withdraw to a prearranged secondary base.

'The intruders must be captured before they leave the sewers,' the Leader intoned in his flat mechanical voice.

'Getting-a-bit-rough-is-it?' Charlie said mimicking the monotone.

Pointing a large, menacing, finger at him, the Leader said: 'Remain silent, or you will die.'

Charlie shrugged. Death no longer seemed a threat; after being taken prisoner by the Cybermen, he had not expected to leave the sewers alive. What had really disturbed him was how readily he had resigned himself to the fact of a sudden demise.

'I shall go ahead and prepare our secondary base,' said the Leader to his Lieutenant. 'I will take a small guard and the two prisoners.'

Charlie nudged Lytton. 'Why are they overreacting?' he whispered. 'No one'll find them here.'

Lytton rubbed a finger along the lid of his left eye as

though massaging the ball beneath. 'They're under-manned,' he said, at last. 'They're not certain, if attacked, they could successfully defend this place.'

'What about help from the ship you mentioned? The dark side of the moon?'

'That is there – they are here.' Confused, Charlie wrinkled his brow. He wasn't very good at deciphering cryptic statements. 'The ship is their only means of getting home. They won't risk losing that to save a group of their own who have failed. What's more, this lot know it.' Lytton glanced around the bustling room. 'I do believe,' he added smugly, 'you, Griffiths, are witnessing a very rare sight indeed – nervous Cybermen.'

As he spoke, two guards lumbered up and ordered them to move. As they approached the door of the base, it silently swung open and they were pushed into a sewer tunnel outside. The Leader, flanked by three guards, followed, and the motley crowd moved off.

The ladder leading from sewer to inspection pit was still in place, but the handcuffed policeman had gone.

'Didn't you cuff him to the ladder?' asked Peri.

The Doctor nodded. 'Never mind about that for the moment.' He steered Peri to the bottom rung. 'Up you go.' Slowly she started to climb. 'Faster than that!' She glared down at the Time Lord and was tempted to do something unpleasant.

'And don't leave the inspection pit until I get there.'

'No, Doctor,' she said, tartly.

'And save your breath for climbing!'

'Yes, Doctor.'

Once Peri was high enough, Russell scrambled onto the ladder. At first he attempted to use his damaged leg, but found it easier to pull himself up on his arms. While Russell struggled, the Doctor ran a little way back along the sewer to act as rearguard.

As he waited in the shadows, listening, he recalled his last encounter with the Cybermen and how his young companion, Adric, had died in an attempt to defeat them. Of all the enemies he had faced, he knew that he despised them most. Even more than the hated Daleks. There was something about their cold, emotionless minds, obsessed with total domination, that put his nerves on edge. He could understand, if not approve, the average tyrant who gloried in power and its manipulation. But the Cybermen glorified in nothing. They had no faith, philosophy or culture of any kind. They didn't make anything useful, other than objects of war. The peoples they defeated were obliterated, and any prisoners taken were turned into emotionless creatures like themselves. Where Cybermen had passed there was always total destruction. Never the briefest moment of compassion shown. Simply death and annihilation.

The Doctor glanced over his shoulder and saw that both Peri and Russell had reached the top of the ladder. Quickly he ran back and climbed up himself, finding his companions, as though under siege in a trench, stooped in the inspection pit.

'No one out there,' muttered Peri. 'Not even the other policeman.'

Cautiously, the Time Lord peered over the edge of the pit. He could see that the part of the cuff attached to the bench was still in place, but the half retaining the policeman's hand had been snapped off at the chain. Knowing this would require enormous strength, he assumed that Cybermen had been in the garage.

This was very bad news indeed, for if the Cybermen had come this far, they might also have entered the TARDIS. Through the open garage door, the Doctor could see his time machine, still in the guise of a pipe organ, parked in the forecourt. Everything seemed quiet, but that was no indication of what could await them inside.

Quietly, as the Doctor briefed them about what might have occurred, the trio climbed out of the pit. Russell untangled, from a deep pocket, the heavy automatic Peri had taken earlier from the uniformed policeman. He gave it to her and then drew the Beretta, checked the contents of the magazine and cocked it. With the Doctor in the lead, the trio made their way to the back of the organ. 'This wasn't here earlier,' said Russell, feeling foolish that he had been asked to creep up on a musical instrument.

'I'll explain later,' the Doctor whispered.

Silently they climbed into the back of the organ, passed through the black, temporal void that separated the outer shell of the TARDIS from its infinite interior and pushed open the console room's double doors.

The Doctor raised the Cyber gun and scanned the empty room. Apart from a tiny light quietly pulsing on the console, everything was still and quiet. The Time Lord let out a slow sigh of relief. Knowing how the Cybermen preferred a stand-up fight, this was where he had expected to encounter them.

So far so good, he thought, edging his way cautiously into the room. This observation had no sooner crackled across his synapse, than a massive metal hand swung round from behind one of the doors and gripped him by the throat. Screaming, he dropped his gun, and tore at the powerful fingers.

In a desperate attempt to break the murderous grip, Russell beat the Cyberman's hand with the butt of his gun, but it remained impervious.

Realising the Doctor had but seconds to live, Russell raised his heavy automatic, aimed at the vent that should have been the Cyberman's mouth and fired. He continued to squeeze the trigger until the gun's magazine was empty and the Cyberman destroyed.

'Careful,' the Time Lord croaked, clutching his bruised neck, 'there might be others.'

Russell picked up the Cyber gun. 'How does this thing work?'

The Doctor pointed at the trigger.

'Look out!' shouted Peri.

Russell turned and saw another Cyberman entering from the internal corridor. Aiming the gun, he fired, and the creature's chest exploded. Russell then hobbled across the room to check that others weren't lurking in the corridor. As he reached the door, a mighty fist seemed to come from nowhere, striking the policeman on the neck. The crack echoed round the room as his spinal cord fractured. Russell died instantly.

'No!' screamed Peri, beginning to sob. 'That wasn't necessary!'

A metal face stared down at her, not comprehending one emotional word she uttered.

Peri continued to sob and sob, but all the tears in the world could not bring the policeman back to life.

In the sewers a curious mouse was examining the remains of the destroyed Cyberman as the Leader and his party arrived. As the mouse scurried away, Lytton noticed the sonic lance protruding from the respirator.

'Do you recognise this, Leader?' he said, extracting it from the wreckage. 'Strange it should be here, especially as Earth technology has yet to develop the sonic lance.'

Staring first at the lance then at Lytton, the Leader asked: 'Where has it come from?'

'I think I know.' Lytton screwed up his face as though having smelt something particularly nasty. 'He calls himself the Doctor. I've been expecting him to return.'

A strange rumble emanated from the Leader's voice box. 'I know that name,' he said. 'He is an enemy of the Cyber race.'

As the Leader spoke a Cyberman stepped forward and informed him of the TARDIS' capture.

'What's a TARDIS?' inquired Charlie.

'A machine capable of travelling in time.'

Charlie shrugged. Why not, he thought. After the events of the last few hours anything was possible – including time travel!

6

Telos

By the time the Cyber Leader's group had reached the TARDIS, Russell's body had been removed from the console room and dumped in an undignified heap in the corridor; and as though to show there wasn't any discrimination, the destroyed Cyberman had been dealt with in a similar fashion.

Peri, her eyes red from crying, stood by the console. She had wrapped her arms around herself, as though in a reassuring self-cuddle, but it hadn't helped. She still felt isolated, scared and very, very unhappy.

Sitting next to her on the floor, the Doctor nursed his bruised neck. He felt very angry, aware that his thoughtlessness had precipitated the current shambles. Both Peri and Russell had advised waiting for help, but he hadn't listened, foolishly preferring to take on a squad of the fiercest warriors in the galaxy. Not only had his folly cost Russell his life, but the TARDIS was now controlled by Cybermen. And as though to endorse his stupidity, Commander Gustave Lytton was glaring at him from the other side of the room, a reminder of yet another major blunder in his life.

As the Leader crossed to where he was sitting, the Doctor, using the edge of the console, pulled himself to his feet. Once upright, he noticed that his fingers were only millimetres from the distress-call button. All he need do was extend an index finger and a signal would be transmitted directly to Gallifrey. Whereas, in the past, his pride had deterred him from involving the High Council of Time Lords, the theft of a TARDIS, and the consequences it could have on the space/time continuum, were far too important. What was more his pride had already cost the life of one man and it was a mistake he was determined not to repeat. As he turned to face the Cyber Leader, he pressed the button, despatching its urgent signal across the Universe.

'So...' intoned the Leader, 'you have once again changed your appearance.'

The Doctor nodded. 'And once again you are attempting to invade Earth. I should have thought you'd have tired of that by now – certainly of the defeats you've always suffered.'

Pressing a red lever on the console, the Leader closed the double doors, sealing the TARDIS from the outside world. 'It won't happen this time,' he said. 'Now that we have the ability to travel in time.'

'Not through my TARDIS!' growled the Doctor. 'It will take forever to learn how it functions.'

'We already have our own time vessel.'

The Time Lord laughed, but it was empty and hollow. The Doctor knew Cybermen did not boast.

Lytton, who was standing by the closed double door, shifted the weight of his body from one foot to the other. 'The Cyber Leader speaks the truth,' he said, matter-of-factly. 'They have a craft on the dark side of the moon.'

'Really.' The Doctor glared at him and foolishly contorted his face into an expression of contempt. The gesture proved as hollow as his laugh. 'I know Cyber technology,' he muttered. 'It will be many years before they are capable of time travel.'

Grabbing the Doctor by his collar, the Leader pushed him towards the navigational section of the console. 'You will learn that I do not lie,' he said. 'Now set the co-ordinates for Telos. The Cyber Controller wishes to speak to you.'

The Doctor didn't respond but inside his head he was reeling. The last time he was on Telos he had *killed* the Controller, sealing him in the labyrinth of his own tombs.

'He's still alive?'

'You did not destroy him, Doctor – he was merely damaged.' Stunned, the Doctor nodded, allowing his head to foolishly bob up and down as though his neck were a spring. 'Now set the co-ordinates!'

The Doctor obeyed and pressed the master control. The TARDIS dematerialised.

The room was dark and cluttered with panels of electronic circuitry. Fibre-optic cables hung from open roundals and their covers were strewn across the floor. This was where the Cyber Leader had locked the Doctor and the others for safe keeping.

In the middle of the debris stood Charlie Griffiths and Peri. Watched by Lytton, the Doctor was pacing up and down. 'This is bad news...' he muttered to himself. '*Very* bad news. How could they have discovered the Laws of Time?'

'They haven't,' said Lytton casually.

The Doctor wasn't certain whether to believe him. 'You said they had a craft on the dark side of the moon.'

'That's right.' Lytton was enjoying the sight of a flustered Time Lord. 'But they didn't build it.'

'So where did they get it?'

'Engine problems forced it to land on Telos. They simply captured it.'

This pleased the Doctor even less. 'So now they have two: one to operate; the other to dismantle for research.' He wrung his hands as he continued to pace up and down. 'There must be a way to stop them. With the ability to travel in time, they'll cause havoc.' The Doctor turned in mid-step to Lytton. 'Have you ever been to Telos?' He shook his head. 'Then how do you know what happened there?'

Lytton's bottom lip quivered, but didn't quite make the full smile. 'Does it matter?' he said, trying to sound enigmatic. 'Be grateful you're still alive.'

Peri was growing tired of their banter. 'I assume this is Commander Lytton?' she said firmly. 'The one who worked for the Daleks?'

The reference to the Daleks seemed momentarily to upset him. 'That wasn't out of choice,' Lytton protested. 'Anyway, that hardly affects the situation now, as I'm plainly not working for the Cybermen. Like you, I'm a prisoner.'

'More likely a spy!' snarled the Doctor.

Peri shrugged in despair. 'Does it really matter?' She was suddenly angry. 'He won't learn very much. And neither will this arguing get us out of our current mess!' The echo of her anger hovered in the air for a moment. 'She's right.' Charlie Griffiths had found his tongue. 'I don't begin to understand what's going on, but if we're going to get out of this alive, we'll have to co-operate.'

Lytton glanced at the Doctor. 'I'm prepared to,' he said. The Time Lord reluctantly nodded his agreement. 'Don't be so grudging,' mocked Lytton. 'I'm a reformed character. You can trust me.'

Inside his head, the Doctor roared with ironic laughter. He would rather trust a wounded speelsnape, the most vicious creature in the Universe, than place one ounce of reliance on a man like Lytton.

In the TARDIS' console room a coded message was in the process of being received from Telos . . .

The Doctor stood in front of an open roundel and fiddled with the wiring inside.

'What are you trying to do?' asked Peri.

'Upset the navigational control.' He gave the panel he was working on a sharp thump. 'If I can distort the co-ordinates by just a fraction of a degree . . .'

'We'd miss Telos?'

'Not quite.'

'Then what's the point?'

'We won't land where the Cybermen want us to. Hopefully that will provide us with a better chance of escape.'

He began to repeatedly hammer at the panel.

'Would this help?' inquired Lytton, pulling the sonic lance from his pocket.

The Doctor snatched it. 'Where did you get this?'

'From where you left it. I wouldn't try sticking it in the Cyber Controller when we reach Telos. I rather fancy he'd snap your hand off.'

The Doctor turned back to the roundel where he was

working. In spite of Lytton's advice, he wouldn't hesitate in using it on the Controller. The loss of a hand would be a small cost to rid the Universe of such a monster.

While the Doctor worked, Charlie grew more anxious. Not only was he worried about his Ma and cat, but what awaited him on the mysterious Telos. He had been scared many times in his life, yet had always managed to preserve a degree of equanimity. Even while waiting to be sentenced, or the time he drove a getaway car with two slow punctures, while being pursued by half the Metropolitan Police, he had felt calmer, more resolved to his situation than he did now. 'How much longer before we reach Telos?'

Almost from habit, rather than with real contempt, Lytton looked down his nose at Griffiths. 'You'll have to ask the pilot,' he said tersely.

Although Charlie had been the butt of countless verbal put-downs, this one bit into him like the flying tip of a whip, and it made him feel very angry. 'I asked you a civil question, *Mr* Lytton.'

'And you got the only available answer.'

Charlie's anger grew. 'You may think me a fool, but I'm getting fed up with the way you talk to me.' Lytton didn't respond. 'I'm also getting sick and tired of being the only one here who doesn't know what's happening!'

'That's about par for the course,' came the dismissive reply.

Charlie clenched the thick fingers of his right hand. One thing he did know something about was fighting, and Lytton knew it.

Having watched the situation grow, but not knowing how to curb it, Peri now stepped between the two men.

'C'mon guys,' she said gently, placing her fingers on Charlie's fist. 'This is no time to be macho.' She felt the fist under her fingers relax.

'Then someone'd better tell me what's going on,' he demanded.

Grabbing Lytton by the arm, Peri steered him towards Charlie. 'Tell him,' she said firmly.

Lytton eyed Charlie's powerful fingers and modulated his tone accordingly. 'There isn't much to tell,' he said. 'As you know, we're on our way to Telos, the Cybermen's home planet.'

'*Adopted* planet,' interrupted the Doctor, turning to face the group. 'If you're going to tell the story, at least get it right.'

Lytton shrugged casually. 'You probably know it better than I do. Perhaps you should continue.'

'As you wish.' The Doctor cleared his throat as if about to embark on a major lecture. 'Originally, Telos was populated by the Cryons,' he said. 'You would have liked the planet in those days . . .'

Peri wasn't in the mood for reminiscences. 'What happened to them?' she asked. 'Did the Cybermen wipe them out?'

He nodded.

'They had no choice.' Lytton sounded slightly defensive. 'There was nowhere else they could go.'

The Doctor looked stony-eyed. 'For heaven's sake, man, the Universe is littered with unpopulated planets!'

'But few with the facilities Telos offered.'

'That's hardly an excuse for destroying a highly sophisticated culture such as the Cryons!'

There was an awkward silence as though they had both run out of conversation.

'Well don't stop now,' said Charlie suddenly. 'What's so important about Telos?'

'Refrigeration.' The word popped out like an expletive.

'Refrigeration?' Charlie repeated slowly, as though not fully understanding the word. 'Seems a strange reason to kill people.'

'Not when you build refrigerated cities with the ingenuity the Cryons did. Mind you,' he added reflectively, 'they needed to as they couldn't live in temperatures above zero.'

Peri chilled at the thought of such an icy existence. 'But why did the Cybermen suddenly need the cold?'

'Hibernation, Peri... For some reason they needed to rest. Don't ask me why.' He waved a hand in the direction of the door. 'You'd have to ask our tin friends for the full story.'

Peri still wasn't satisfied. 'It doesn't make sense,' she persisted. 'Why didn't they hibernate on their own planet?'

The Doctor glanced awkwardly at Lytton.

'Well...?' she urged, sensing there was something wrong.

'That's right...' Charlie echoed Peri's concern. 'What's going on?'

And for the third time that day, Lytton's face cracked to produce a smile. 'Yes, Doctor,' he grinned, knowing the embarrassment involved, 'what *is* the matter...?'

In the console room, the Cyber Leader had just finished reading the coded message from his base on Telos. 'Fetch the Time Lord,' he hissed to a guard. 'Fetch him at once...'

*

Peri stood in front of the Doctor with arms folded across her chest. 'Well?' she insisted. 'We're all waiting.'

Again he cleared his throat, this time with far less confidence. 'It's a complicated story,' he mumbled.

Peri smiled. 'But I'm sure you can explain it simply.'

The Doctor scowled at her. 'Mondas,' he said awkwardly, 'was the Cybermen's planet.'

Lytton interupted mischievously. 'Tell them what happened to it,' he said.

'I'm coming to that!'

'Tell them how it was destroyed.'

The Doctor ground his teeth and angrily contorted his face, the only effect being to make Lytton laugh. 'You're enjoying this,' he growled.

'It's not often I have the opportunity to watch a time Lord squirm.'

Peri was becoming annoyed. 'Are you going to tell me what happened to Mondas, Doctor?' He didn't want to. 'Well...?' she insisted.

'It blew up.'

'How?'

The Doctor didn't reply.

'It blew up while attacking Earth.' There was a certain gleeful tone in Lytton's voice. 'That's why he didn't want to tell you.'

The Time Lord was angry. 'Take no notice of him,' he urged. 'He's just trying to unnerve you. Your planet survived the attack.'

But Peri wouldn't be distracted. 'Then why were you reluctant to tell us?'

Embarrassed, he turned away. 'I didn't want to upset you.'

Lytton snorted. 'Ask him when the attack happened.'

The Doctor glared at Lytton, and for a moment was tempted to stick the sonic lance in him.

'Well, Doctor?' she demanded.

He tried to prevaricate, but Peri remained insistent. 'Nineteen eighty-six,' he muttered.

Charlie was horrified. 'That's next year!'

As simple arithmetic mitigated against him, there was little the Doctor could do but agree.

'There must be something you can do,' urged Peri forcefully. 'Inform Earth? Tell them what's going to happen?'

He waved a hand, indicating the locked door. 'From here?' the Doctor shook his head. 'How can I do anything? I'm a prisoner.'

Lytton tut-tutted. 'Even if you were free you couldn't transgress the Laws of Time. The High Council of Gallifrey would destroy you if you did.'

The Doctor put his arm gently around Peri's shoulder. 'Don't worry about it. Earth survived with minimal damage. It's an historical fact.'

After having done so well, Charlie had finally lost the thread of the conversation. 'How can it be an historical fact when it hasn't happened yet?'

Lytton despaired. 'It's part of the Web of Time,' he said. 'It's always happened; always will happen; the Universe would be destroyed if it didn't happen. Do you understand now?' Frantically, Charlie shook his head. 'It's the same with the Cryons: they have always been destroyed, as they must and always will be.'

Charlie still didn't understand. In his mind history always meant the past. However Lytton turned it upside down, it would always remain so. It had to. For Charlie was confused enough without having to cope with the reversal of received concepts. If he were to escape from his current situation with any degree of sanity, he had to hang on to his own little world, however banal it might appear to others.

'I don't understand how history can be in the future,' he said dismally, 'but can someone explain how a planet can travel around off its orbit, 'cause when I was at school that sort of thing didn't happen. At least not in the CSE General Science I took and failed.'

'It had a propulsion unit,' said the Doctor.

The answer was so obvious it made Charlie feel like a fool. But before he could ask a supplementary question, the door was thrown open and two Cybermen marched in.

'You will come with me,' said the first Cyberman, gripping Peri by the arm.

'Why?'

'Go with him,' urged the Doctor. 'This isn't the time to be difficult.'

The second Cyberman grabbed the Doctor and pushed him towards the door. 'No need for the rough stuff,' said the Doctor. 'Just say where you want me to go, and I'll manage to get there all by myself.'

But the Cyberman wasn't listening and harshly pushed the Doctor into the corridor.

The door of the console room burst open and the Doctor was thrown in. As he scrambled to his feet, two Cybermen moved behind him and each grabbed an arm and shoulder.

'Is all this violence necessary?'

'You have deceived us, Doctor,' said the Leader.

The Cybermen started to squeeze his shoulders, their

metal finger cutting deep into his flesh.

'What have I done?' he screamed.

The Leader didn't answer, allowing him to suffer for a little while, and through his pain, to contemplate his crimes against the Cyber race.

'Please tell me what you want,' begged the Time Lord.

'You will disconnect the signal you are transmitting.'

In his agony all the Doctor could manage was a brief nod. The Cybermen loosened their grip and pushed him towards the console. 'First tell me what you've done with Peri.'

'She is unharmed,' rasped the Leader. 'Telos is cold. She must have warmer clothing.'

Satisfied he was being told the truth, the Doctor disconnected the distress signal and stepped back from the console. 'It's done,' he said, massaging his shoulders.

The Leader gave a small nod and one of the Cybermen guards hit the Doctor, sending him crashing across the console room and into the wall. Then slowly, very slowly, the stunned Time Lord slithered down it.

The sounds of excavation echoed across the bleak, barren surface of the planet Telos. In a small, disused quarry a dozen men worked, clawing at the iron-hard ground with picks, shovels and crude hand-operated drilling devices. Although the work was painfully gruelling, they worked effortlessly, as though impervious to tiredness. This was not because of the Cyberguards, who patrolled the ridge above them, but because their arms and legs had been Cybernised. Instead of muscle and bone, they had powerful hydraulic, robotic limbs.

The men worked on, drilling into the ground, then

loading the hole with explosives and a radio operated detonator. Then they moved on, repeating the operation. For three weeks they had worked like this, criss-crossing the planet's surface with narrow pits of impending destruction. It was the intention of the Cybermen to destroy the massive tombs that existed beneath the surface.

Stratton and Bates, two of the men in the gang, were aware of this plan and also knew that all non-Cybermen, like themselves, would be left behind to perish. As such a demise did not appeal, they had decided to do something about it.

Flight Leader Lintus Stratton and Time Navigator Eregous Bates came from the planet Hatre Sedtry in the star system known as Repton's Cluster. In size, geological and meteorological terms it was a planet not dissimilar to Earth. The inhabitants were very similar in appearance too, being biped male and females with all the attributes of mammalian life forms. Apart from cultural differences, the other main dissimilitude was in their technology – they were many thousands of years ahead of Earth. Such were their advanced skills they had proceeded well beyond the incipient stages of developing a ship which could travel through the time/space continuum. It was while Bates and Stratton had been flight-testing the craft that they had crash landed on Telos. Not only had their flight engineer been killed, but they had been captured by Cybermen. Forced to repair their craft, then instruct them how to operate it, they had been rewarded by being subjected to Cybernisation. But the processing had partially failed and only their arms and legs had been altered. Rather than destroy them, the Cybermen sent them to work on the slave demolition gangs. But now Bates and Stratton plotted to humiliate their captors by stealing back their craft and making good their escape. The only problem was they needed a third man to help them crew the vessel. Even though luck had been on their side, and a member of the slave gang admitted to flight experience, they had to spend many long hours briefing him on the complications of time travel.

But now they were ready to go.

Stratton glanced up at the four Cybermen spaced along the ridge above them. A fifth had just descended into the quarry to examine a problem with the drill.

Stratton nodded to Bates, who acknowledged the signal. As the Cyberman passed in front of Stratton, he lifted his shovel and swung it with such force he decapitated the guard, sending the head flying towards his friend.

Bates stood frozen to the spot, staring at the smoking head.

'Run!' screamed Stratton.

Bates still didn't move.

The Cyberguards on the ridge raised their guns ready for action. As they did, another member of the gang took to his heels, but was immediately shot down.

Panic broke out as others ran for cover. In the confusion, Stratton was able to escape, dragging a terrified Bates behind him.

Once they were clear of the quarry, and satisfied they weren't being followed, the two men rested.

Still bemused by the suddenness of events, Bates looked around him. 'Where's the other chap?' he said. 'The one who was to act as third crew member.'

Stratton let out a loud sigh of frustration and

momentarily buried his face in his hands. 'He's dead!' He spat out the words. 'And all because you froze!' Stratton was now on the verge of hitting Bates. 'Even if we can get back to our craft, there is no way we can fly it by ourselves.'

Bates stared down at the dry, dusty ground. 'You shouldn't have killed the guard as you did,' he muttered in mitigation. 'I'm not a soldier or used to fighting.'

Stratton scrambled to his feet. 'Then you'd better learn,' he shouted, 'because we're now at war with the Cybermen!'

Bates stood up and looked back the way they had come. 'They're not following.'

'That's because they know where we're going.' He grabbed Bates by the collar of his insulated suit and dragged him to the next ridge. 'You see that?' he said, pointing. 'That's where we have to go.'

Bates focused on the huge building that rose out of the bleak landscape a couple of kilometres away.

'That's Cyber Control,' said Stratton. 'That's where our ship is ... And that's where the Cyber Controller has thousands of guards ... just waiting for us to arrive!'

Bates blinked at the thought and wondered whether he really wanted to escape.

7

The Tombs of the Cybermen

The endless corridors, with their tiny sepulchres every few metres, each containing a Cyberman in hibernation, stretched almost to beyond imagination. Everywhere was cold and bleak and covered in thick layers of hard frost. Yet in spite of the frozen atmosphere, the sour stench of decay was everywhere.

In a small gallery, deep in the heart of the labyrinth, the familiar sound of the TARDIS was heard. A moment later a large baroque portal materialised that was just as out of place as its previous attempts at camouflage. Cautiously its door opened and the Cyber Leader emerged, flanked by two guards.

Looking around, he rubbed a metal finger across a frozen wall, gouging a deep furrow in the frost. Something had gone wrong. Turning to one of the guards, he ordered him to contact Cyber Control and report on the situation.

Escorted by a Cyberman, the Doctor – still a little groggy from his beating – followed by Peri, Lytton and Charlie Griffiths, stumbled into the frozen corridor. It wasn't long before they began to stamp their feet and rub their hands in large, exaggerated movements, and mutter obvious remarks about the temperature like frustrated passengers waiting for a bus on a cold winter's morning. Charlie, always keen to lighten the atmosphere, attempted to blow rings with the billow of his steamy breath, but no one was interested. Instead they wanted to huddle in a tight bunch in an attempt to maintain the rapidly decreasing warmth in their bodies.

'So this is Telos,' Charlie muttered. 'I must say I've had more fun with toothache.'

Lytton glanced over his shoulder of the Leader, who was in deep conversation with one of the guards. 'Seems almost concerned,' he observed. 'As though we've landed in the wrong place.'

The Doctor grinned in a childish, self-satisfied way.

Shivering, Peri plunged her hands, with more force than necessary, deep into the cavities of her armpits. 'I should have guessed you were responsible for this,' she growled through chattering teeth. 'Only *you* could find such an unpleasant place.'

Suddenly a Cyberman pushed the huddled group towards the Leader with the point of his gun. Grumbling, they moved as directed.

'We must leave this place at once,' he said. 'There is danger.'

Danger? Peri and Charlie exchanged quizzical glances and assumed he meant the cold.

Leaving a Cyberman to guard the TARDIS – the Doctor wondered from what or whom – the group trudged off on their long, cold journey to Cyber Control.

Only Lytton knew the full truth of the situation, and as far as he was concerned, everything was going as planned.

*

Not only did the corridors seem to go on forever, but their total uniformity did nothing to alleviate the frustration and boredom of their trek. What was more, the temperature seemed to be dropping, making each step more and more painful. Even Charlie, who was tougher and fitter than the others, found the going hard. What was more, his boots had started to pinch again.

'Can we rest?' asked the Doctor.

The Leader raised a hand and the group came to a shuddering halt. 'We cannot delay for long,' he said.

Everyone was so tired that even the briefest pause was a pleasure, and they duly muttered their grateful thanks.

After brushing frost from her eyebrows, Peri then vigorously rubbed her frozen cheeks and chin. As she worked she became aware of a strong odour. 'What's that terrible smell?' Her mouth was numb and she could hardly form the words.

Charlie sniffed the air. To him it smelt like an old foxfur his gran used to wear. Knowing this was an unlikely explanation, he decided to remain silent.

'It's death,' intoned Lytton.

Peri almost skidded on a patch of ice. 'What do you mean – death?'

'It's sour stench is unmistakable.'

Trust him to cheer everyone up, thought Charlie.

Peri turned to the Doctor. 'You said the Cybermen were hibernating?'

The Time Lord shrugged. 'I did,' he said, staring at Lytton. 'But I think our friend knows far more than he's prepared to tell us.'

Lytton didn't reply, and somehow managed to form an expression of deep esotericism. The Doctor was impressed. It required enormous skill to blend such a look with that of his usual enigmatic mask. If nothing else, thought the Doctor, Commander Gustave Lytton certainly knew how to be a Man of Mystery.

The Cyber Leader's respirator suddenly let out a loud rasp. Peri noticed that a small circle of frost, like an intricate lace doily, had formed on his forehead. 'We must leave at once!' he instructed.

'Sounds concerned,' whispered Peri.

The Doctor couldn't deny it, and wondered whether modern Cybermen were now programmed with limited emotional response.

As the group prepared to move off, the source of the Leader's urgency became apparent. Suddenly there was an enormous, penetrating roar from within a nearby sepulchre, like a huge monster in terminal distress. The bellow grew louder and more frightening. As the Cybermen raised their guns, a powerful metal fist smashed through the door of the tomb. Such was its speed, it caught a guard unawares, grasping him by the neck. A second hand immediately followed and, gripping the head, ripped it from his shoulders. Smoke and sparks poured from the fractured neck as the guard's body was hurled to one side. A moment later, the crypt door was torn from its tracks, and in the opening stood a slime-covered Cyberman, emitting a sound like a soul in agony. The Leader opened fire and the tormented creature died.

Seeing their chance of escape, the Doctor pushed Peri on her way. 'Run!' he screamed.

Peri hesitated, waiting for the Doctor to follow.

'Don't wait for me – GO!'

The Cyberguard turned, and seeing Peri, raised his gun to fire. Quickly the Time Lord shoulder-charged him, managing to deflect his aim. As the bolt of laser energy hissed past her head, Peri turned and ran as she had never done before.

During the confusion Lytton had also taken his chance, and grabbing Griffiths by the arm, had pulled him along a nearby side-passage and into an already opened tomb.

The Doctor, now held by the guard, watched helplessly as he raised a mighty fist. Although he struggled with all his strength, he couldn't break the powerful grip holding him.

'Wait!' ordered the Leader. 'He must not be harmed.'

Slowly, almost reluctantly, the guard lowered his hand. Such was the Time Lord's terror, it was a full minute before he could sigh with relief.

Breathlessly Peri ran into a long gallery that seemed to go on forever. She stopped and leant against the wall trying to recapture her breath. It's pointless to continue, she thought. Must re-orientate myself.

To help concentrate her thoughts, she closed her eyes, but the silence was awesome and overpowering. And now that she was alone, the cold seemed to bite even deeper. *Why not have a nap*, a voice whispered. *Lie down for a few minutes. It will do you nothing but good.* She knew that to obey would mean certain death. *You'll find the ground soft and comfortable*, the voice persisted. *A short rest will restore your strength.* I must keep moving, she thought. Generate heat and clear the phantom voice from my mind. Summoning up her last reserves of energy, she struggled to open her eyes. *Lie down and rest,* the voice purred convincingly. *It won't do you any harm.* Slowly her mind began to obey and she drifted into sleep. *That's right*, it urged. *Now you'll feel much better.*

Slowly warmth flooded back into her limbs, generating a satisfied feeling of contentment. She no longer felt hungry, afraid or alone. She was suddenly with friends, who beckoned her to join them. Peri started to run, waving and calling... but now they seemed further away. She increased her speed, calling louder...

But suddenly, in the distance, on the fringe of her warmth and security, she heard another familar sound. The voice, which now dominated her mind, urged her to disregard it. But Peri sensed an overpowering feeling of danger. Clawing at the fringes of reality, she slowly dragged herself back. As she did, she heard the noise again, only this time much louder. What was it? she thought. Why was it so familiar?

Then suddenly the truth filled her mind, and she was wide awake – her warmth and comfort gone. Next to her, having punched his way through the door of his tomb, flayed a pair of slime-covered Cyberman's arms. Peri tried not scream, but exhaustion and fear prevented its containment. As her panic exploded, each cry seemed to generate yet further pairs of arms, as other entombed Cybermen attempted to punch their way to freedom...

At last one succeeded.

Peri, too exhausted to run, stood helplessly in his path as he lurched towards her. As consciousness slipped from her mind, she thought she saw two white shapes fire a finger of flame at her attacker, but the shutter of darkness closed before she could be certain...

Charlie followed Lytton blindly along a dark tunnel. How Lytton had known it was there more than puzzled him.

Suddenly the tunnel blossomed into a large cave illuminated by small white globes.

'Come on,' urged Lytton. 'Keep moving.'

'Hang on.' Charlie ground to a stubborn, deliberate halt. 'Where do you think you're going?'

'Taking you home...' Lytton indicated ahead. 'Back to Earth.'

Charlie wasn't impressed. 'Oh, I see,' he said sarcastically. 'You gotta taxi waiting?'

'I have something better.' Lytton walked on.

As Charlie ran to catch him up, he saw a figure step from behind a rock. It was small and slim like a youth or young woman and was wearing what appeared to be a very close-fitting white jump suit.

'What's *that?*' he exclaimed.

Lytton raised a hand in greeting. 'That, my dear Griffiths, is a Cryon.'

As the figure approached, Charlie could see that the creature was similar in build to that of an Earth woman. The face, on the other hand, was quite different. Covered in a translucent membrane, with large bulbous eyes, the lower half sprouted what looked like course white hair.

The Cryon raised her hand in an identical greeting to the one given by Lytton. 'My name is Thrust...' The voice was high-pitched, but not unpleasant. And unlike a Cyberman's, contained personality and cadence. 'Welcome, Lytton.'

Charlie couldn't believe what he had heard. 'She *knows* you!'

'Of course,' the Cryon said pleasantly. 'Lytton has come to help us.'

Charlie turned to him. 'What's all this about?' he

whispered frantically. 'How can you know her?'

Commander Gustave Lytton cleared his throat and reminded Charlie about the robbery at the electronics factory. He explained he had built a transmitter from stolen components capable of slipping a signal through the gaps in the space/time continuum. The Cryons had received his transmission and told him about the Cybermen on Earth.

'And now you are both here to help us defeat the Cybermen,' added Thrust.

BOTH! Charlie screamed inside his head.

'I haven't told Griffiths about his part yet.'

Charlie was furious. 'I was brought here on purpose!' he exclaimed. Lytton nodded. 'You never did intend to do that diamond job.'

'Would you have come if I'd told you the truth?'

'You bet I wouldn't!'

Thrust stepped between the two men. 'We realise this must be confusing for you.' Her tone was sweet and placating. 'But Lytton didn't lie: there is a way to get home . . .'

Mendacity was a stock in trade for most crooks, and therefore something even the beginner quickly learned to access. But Charlie had been told so many lies in the last couple of days, he no longer knew what to believe. 'All right,' he said at last. 'Convince me.'

The gaze from her large, round eyes seemed to bore into his brain. 'First we must discuss the fee for your services.'

He grunted his disapproval, knowing that his high street bank would react with a telephone call to the nearest psychiatric hospital, should he present them with a cheque drawn on the Bank of Telos. 'Are you trying to wind me up?'

Thrust didn't understand the colloquialism and referred to Lytton. 'He implies that you're attempting to annoy him.'

Aghast, she waved her hands. 'Certainly not,' she said, tugging at a pouch stuffed into her waistband. 'That is the last thing I should want to do.' She handed the bag to Charlie.

'Approximately two million pounds in uncut diamonds,' said Lytton, watching him open the leather container and empty the contents into his hand.

'We were surprised you should want so little,' she demurred. 'Diamonds are common on Telos.'

Turning the stones over in his hand, Charlie wondered how many atrocities he would have to commit to earn such a wage.

'You will help us?' simpered the Cryon.

He didn't know what to think. 'What've I got to do?'

Lytton grinned broadly. 'Help me steal back a time vessel.'

Before meeting the Doctor, the Cyber Controller had decided to humiliate his prisoner, hoping to soften his will to resist. It was to this end that the Time Lord had been thrown into a massive refrigeration unit.

Cold and desperate, the Doctor peered into the gloom around him . . .

'A time vessel,' Charlie Griffiths was incredulous. 'You gotta be out of your mind!' He anxiously rubbed the back of his neck, and in spite of the freezing atmosphere, found he was perspiring. 'Me fly a ship! I mean, I'm none too clever behind the wheel of a car!'

'It isn't necessary for you to pilot the ship,' said the Cryon. 'A crew is being assembled for that.'

'Your function, as always, Griffiths, is muscle: you're to keep me alive,' said Lytton.

'A minder?'

Thrust didn't understand.

'A bodyguard,' said Lytton.

The Cryon again waved her hands as though conducting an imaginery orchestra. 'An honourable profession,' she exclaimed.

Charlie wasn't so certain. 'But why me? Why can't one of your lot do it?'

Thrust shrugged and looked disappointed. 'I wish we could,' she said. 'But we can only exist at temperatures below zero. If I were to venture onto the surface of the planet, I would boil and die.'

Lytton was becoming impatient. 'Come on, Griffiths. You are being paid two million pounds for what will be little more than a day's work.'

'But will I live to spend it?' he retorted.

'If we capture the vessel – yes.'

'And if we don't?'

'Then we'll be turned into emotionless Cybermen!'

Not much of a choice, he thought. But that, in many respects, had been the story of his life. At least this time he would have enough money to retire.

Rattling the diamonds in his hand to reassure himself they were real, he finally agreed. Thrust, who was delighted, literally danced for joy. She then took them to where she had hidden a captured Cyber gun, a small backpack containing provisions and an electronic device fitted with a tiny monitor screen.

'A safe route has been plotted to the site of the time

vessel,' she said holding up the box. 'But first you must locate the rest of your crew.'

The Cryon pressed a button on the device then handed it to Lytton. On its tiny screen appeared a relief map of the area near Cyber Control. 'You'll find them somewhere out there,' she said, pointing. 'But now you must hurry. There is very little time!'

Peri lay on a hard stone ledge covered in a foul-smelling blanket. Neither of these inconveniences bothered her very much as she was still unconscious.

Around her prone shape, the Cryons bustled. Although the area was little more than a cave, it was crammed full with electronic monitoring equipment, most of which had been stolen from the Cybermen. The area of the tombs was displayed on a myriad screen, including the landing place of the TARDIS. On another monitor was a gallery through which Lytton and Charlie Griffiths were being led by Thrust. On yet another was the entrance to the refrigeration unit in which the Doctor had been imprisoned.

Slowly Peri began to regain consciousness. Varne and Rost, who were working nearby, heard her groan. Peri's eyelid fluttered, then opened lazily, but all she could see was a dense, myopic haze. As her other senses began to take in the sounds and smells about her, she struggled to focus her vision. Slowly hard edges began to form around the blurred shapes, and she saw the faces of Rost and Varne looking curiously down at her. At first she didn't know what to think, her aching brain desperately trying to make sense of what she saw. It wasn't until Varne's bulging eyes blinked, and Rost pressed an icy finger against her cheek, that Peri sensed danger.

Screaming, she sat bolt upright.

'Peace, child,' said Rost gently. 'We mean you no harm.'

Peri kicked the smelly blanket from around her legs and tried to stand up.

'We saved you from the Cybermen,' said Varne, attempting to restrain her. 'Surely you remember?'

Peri stopped struggling as her memory allowed the incident to filter back into her conscious mind. 'I'm s-sorry,' she stuttered nervously. 'I'm very confused.'

Rost picked up the blanket. 'You must rest,' she said, wrapping it around her. 'We can talk later...'

But Peri was so wide awake she felt that she would never sleep again. 'Who are you?' she demanded.

Rost and Varne glanced at each other. 'We are Cryons, child.'

'How can that be?' Peri mentally kicked herself for such an unthinking reply. 'I mean –' she stammered ineffectually. 'Well, er...'

'You seem perplexed, child,' teased Rost.

Vigorously she shook her head. 'No, no, not at all.'

Varne let out a high-pitched squeal: the Cryon's form of laughing. 'Someone has told of our nation's demise,' she brayed.

Peri's cheeks flushed and she looked embarrassed.

'Ask the Cybermen if *all* the Cryons have been destroyed!' She let out another shrill squeak. 'Then ask them to show you their dead, for *that* bears witness to the fact we live!'

Other Cryons in the cave began to laugh and let out strange little cheers. Although it was all meant to be in good humour, the slightly fanatical tone in Varne's voice, and the over-reaction from the other Cryons concerned

107

Peri. She knew that she would have to escape as soon as possible.

The refrigeration area was staked with hundreds of sealed boxes. As much for something to do as out of curiosity, the Doctor had tried to force one open, but with little success. Now his fingers were severely chilled and although he had worked hard to warm them, he feared that they were in the initial stages of frostbite.

Hammering on the door, the Doctor shouted to be let out.

'They won't answer,' said a very tired voice. 'At least they never have for me.'

The Doctor turned and saw a grotesquely disfigured Cryon slowly making her way between two high pillars of stacked cases. 'Ah,' he said nervously, surprised by her sudden arrival. 'How do you do. I'm the Doctor.'

'My name is Flast.' She lifted her hand in a Cryon greeting. 'Welcome.' Her voice sounded weak, as though exhausted by the effort of walking. 'I'm truly sorry that you are a prisoner.' She let out a terrible gasp and lowered herself onto a nearby box.

'Are you all right?'

The Cryon sighed. 'Do not fret for me, Doctor. I know that I am nearly dead.' Quickly he crossed to where she was seated, but she raised a hand indicating that he should not touch her. 'Look at me.' She pointed at her savagely scarred face. 'Once I was considered beautiful.' The tip of a finger settled onto a gouge running the length of her face. 'The Cybermen did this to me. They have tortured me for what seems like forever, but I have not betrayed any secrets.'

The Time Lord placed a comforting hand on her

108

shoulder. 'Cryons are known throughout the galaxy for their bravery,' he said kindly.

Flast was surprised. 'You know that I am a Cryon?' He nodded. 'Cybermen propaganda has attempted to convince the Universe of our extinction.'

He smiled and said reassuringly: 'And failed! No one ever believes the feeble attempts at inculcation practised by Cybermen.'

Flast started to cough, her ruined lungs rasping as they expelled air. 'It is only a matter of time before their message of hate becomes the truth,' she wheezed. 'There are very few of us left... I fear we are a dying breed.'

The Time Lord began to pace up and down. 'Sorry about having to charge around like this,' he said, blowing out clouds of steamy breath, 'but if I don't keep moving, I'll freeze to the spot.'

The Cryon understood. 'I thought you were looking a little blue.'

'I am: both cold and depressed!'

She gave a small chuckle which deteriorated into another coughing fit. 'I think I shall enjoy your company,' she managed to gasp, once the turmoil in her lungs had subsided.

As he crossed to the door, the Doctor wondered who would expire first: himself from hypothermia; or Flast from bronchial collapse.

The Cryon watched as the Time Lord examined a metal plate attached to the wall alongside an upright jamb. Knowingly, she shook her head. 'Ah, you now dream of escape,' she said wistfully. 'They all do that to begin with... But then they become depressed... It's the locked door and armed guard that's the unsolvable problem.'

The Doctor wasn't deterred. 'There must be a way,' he said firmly, 'for *both* of us.'

'It's too late for me.' Her tone was now mournful. 'I hate the Cybermen more than you could ever know, but my days of fighting them are over.'

'From the stench of death everywhere, there may not be much more fighting to do.' Taking out a handkerchief he wiped a thick deposit of frost from the metal plate. 'I assume you and your people are responsible for the highly disturbed behaviour of certain entombed Cybermen?'

She nodded. 'But the Cryons will not be satisfied until the Cyber Controller is dead.'

The Doctor agreed. 'Especially now they have the ability to time travel.'

Satisfied that the door-opening mechanism was housed behind the plate, he turned back to Flast. 'It's their ignorance which concerns me most,' he said, rubbing his hands together like a demented person. 'Misuse of a time vessel could irreparably damage the Web of Time.'

'That is what they intend to do.'

'How?'

'You know about Mondas, Doctor?'

'The Cybermen's original planet ... yes.' The Time Lord was becoming agitated.

'It was destroyed ...'

He already knew that. 'So?'

Flast's chest heaved with the effort of speaking. 'They intend to change history.'

The Doctor momentarily closed his eyes; he felt sick. 'How?' he asked, praying quietly she would not give the anticipated answer.

But she did.

'Mondas will not be destroyed as it always has been. The Cyber Controller has decreed it.'

Too stunned to answer, the Doctor simply stared ahead into the gloom. He could not believe the proposed stupidity. Mondas had always been destroyed. For it not to happen would wreck the Web of Time, with disastrous repercussions affecting every corner of the Universe. The thought was almost too awful to consider. Billions would die; major civilisations instantly disappear. The Doctor wasn't even certain the fabric of the Universe could withstand such an upheaval.

Regaining his composure, he questioned Flast closely concerning her extraordinary statement, but she remained adamant.

'I couldn't invent such a story,' she protested.

He knew she was telling the truth. It would require the kind of emotionless, uncaring mind of a Cyberman to think up such a diabolically destructive plan.

And that was precisely what the Cyber Controller had done . . .

8

The Great Escape

The star which provided Telos with heat and light had
started to set. Another day was coming to an end. From
the north a chilly wind had begun to blow causing spirals
of grey dust to eddy across the planet's surface. Now that
the work parties engaged in laying explosives had
returned to base, the terrain seemed bleak and devoid of
all life.

At least that was how it felt to Charlie Griffiths and
Commander Gustave Lytton as they pushed open a
heavy grille leading to the planet's surface.

'We must be out of our minds,' moaned Charlie as he
stepped into the swirling dust. 'We'll never find them.'

Closing the grille cover, Lytton ordered him to move
off. Then taking out the electronic device supplied by the
Cryon, he switched it on.

'How will that help?' asked Charlie.

'Not only will it lead us to the time vessel, but it also
detects the presence of Cybermen.'

Suddenly scared, Charlie looked around. 'Are those
things out here as well?'

'Like your worst fears and fantasies,' teased Lytton,

'they are everywhere.'

Charlie was not amused. He had always thought Lytton did not possess a sense of humour, and now Lytton had started to deliver the occasional quip, Charlie decided he preferred the less droll side of his nature.

They trudged on, their long spidery shadows dancing before them. As they neared a hillock, a tiny neon began to flash indicating the presence of Cybermen. Lytton nudged Charlie to show him the warning light. He then slipped the machine quickly into his pocket and unshouldered the Cyber gun.

'Hold it!' a voice boomed. 'Throw down the weapon.'

Charlie was surprised that it wasn't the flat, emotionless tones of a Cyberman.

Lytton did as instructed, then both he and Charlie raised their hands. Behind them they heard two pairs of feet scrambling down the hillock. It was Stratton and Bates.

'Don't turn round,' commanded Stratton.

A moment later rough hands were frisking Charlie in the search for concealed weapons. 'This one's flesh and blood!' exclaimed Stratton, prodding Charlie in the chest. He then searched Lytton. 'So is he.'

'What's he talking about?' muttered Charlie. 'He isn't a Cyberman.' But then he remembered the flashing light. '*Is he?*'

'Almost,' said Lytton.

'You want to see what Cybermen do?' Stratton snarled.

While Bates picked up the Cyber gun, Stratton removed a glove then rolled up his tunic sleeve, revealing a robotic arm.

Feeling suddenly ill, Charlie stared at the wire tendons

and metal bones. 'How much of you is ...' His voice trailed away as though too embarrassed to go on.

'Arms and legs.' The sleeve was rolled down. 'Their conditioning process doesn't always work, so you finish up only partially Cybernised.'

'You mean you're sort of rejects?'

Bates grunted. 'That's one way of putting it.'

Charlie felt even worse. 'Will they do that to me?'

'Only if we're caught,' said Lytton smugly. 'And I don't intend to let that happen.'

'What makes you so certain?' sniggered Stratton. 'We had no problems in taking you.'

'That's because I wanted you to.'

'Oh, yeah,' he jeered.

Lytton smiled. 'We're here to help you ...'

Neither of the men could believe his arrogance, but Lytton ploughed on regardless. 'What if I tell you we want to help you steal back your time vessel?'

Suddenly the jeering stopped and Bates angrily jabbed the gun into Lytton's back. 'Who told you we're after that?' he demanded.

'You *are* Stratton and Bates?' Their expressions answered for them. 'There's no mystery how I know who you are,' he continued. 'The Cryons told me.' Lytton was back in control of the situation. 'I also know they encouraged you to escape. And since the third member of your crew was killed, I am here to help you operate your ship.'

Stratton shifted his feet uneasily. 'We don't need you.'

Lytton pulled the electronic device from his pocket. 'I think you do,' he said, holding it up.

Bates snatched it. 'What is it?'

'It contains a safe route to your ship.' Slowly Lytton

114

lowered his aching arms, knowing that if they accepted his story, he would not be asked to raise them again.

'All right,' said Bates, handing back the device, 'show us.' He pointed his gun at Lytton's head. 'But any tiny hint of deception and you're both dead.' Charlie gulped in a silly, melodramatic fashion. 'Now lead on!'

Charlie and Lytton turned back to face both the grille and the wind. Now behind them, their thin, spindly shadows appeared like sinister, mocking spectres waiting to witness death. Slowly, as though suddenly very tired, the four men moved off.

Apart from wanting to escape, Peri was also becoming concerned about the Doctor. For all she knew he was dead, killed by a marauding Cyberman. If that were so she could be trapped on Telos for the rest of her life. The thought did not appeal, especially as the climate was so cold.

Peri started to scan the enormous bank of monitors. As they seemed to cover almost every part of the underground city, she wondered if they could locate her friend. Cautiously she ambled to where Varne and Rost were working at a nearby console. On a VDU she saw the mighty portal that was the TARDIS' current image. 'Hey!' she said pointing at the screen. 'That's where we landed.'

Varne watched as Rost again played the mother-hen. 'Come, child,' she bustled. 'You should be resting.'

Peri resisted being herded back to her ledge. 'There isn't time,' she protested. 'I have a friend – the Doctor. I need to know if he's safe.'

Varne punched up the image of the Time Lord onto a screen. 'He's alive, but in Cyber Control,' she said.

Peri was delighted. 'Could we rescue him?'

Varne shook her head. 'To enter that place would mean certain death.'

Turning from the screen, Peri walked back dejectedly to where she had been sitting. 'What about the other people I arrived with?'

'They are in the tombs,' lied Varne. 'We are searching for them now.'

Sitting down, she pulled the blanket tightly around her. She felt sad and miserable. The nightmare that she might one day be trapped on an alien planet was on the verge of being realised. Not knowing what to do, she began to review recent events. Everything seemed to have happened so quickly that she felt confused about everything. It wasn't until she looked up and saw the frozen image of the Doctor on the screen that she realised something was wrong. Peri jumped up. 'When I mentioned the Doctor, how did you know who he was?'

Varne played with a switch pretending to be deeply involved with some problem. 'What do you mean, child?'

'I arrived with three men,' she protested. 'Yet you immediately knew who I wanted.'

Rost looked awkwardly at Varne. 'You never were very bright,' she muttered.

Varne turned away. 'We should have killed her,' she said coyly. 'Then I shouldn't need to be.'

Peri was furious. 'You know more than you're saying.'

Like an Edwardian paterfamilias, Varne awkwardly twiddled a lock of coarse hair on her upper lip.

Rost simply looked nervous.

'Well?' demanded Peri. 'I'm waiting for an answer.' But she didn't really need one, having guessed the truth.

'You know Lytton, don't you?' Reluctantly Rost nodded. 'But the man's a criminal!'

'For what we wish him to do,' said Varne, 'that is an excellent qualification.'

This was another revelation. 'He's *working* for you?'

Rost placed her arm around Peri's shoulder. 'You must not prejudge him,' she said gently. 'Lytton has a most important mission – to prevent the Cybermen leaving Telos.'

Peri shrugged the arm away. 'I thought you would have been glad to see them go.'

Rost's face was engulfed with a look of utter despair. 'On their departure,' she said angrily, 'they will destroy our refrigeration units. That is what Lytton must stop!'

Having just learned of her own planet's impending war, she could more than empathise with the Cryons. But from what the Doctor had told her about Lytton, she couldn't help but wonder whether they had made the right choice of knight errant.

The Doctor lumbered about his icy cold prison. Not only was he numbed by the cold, but also by the Cybermen's intention. 'Have you any idea how they intend to destroy Earth?'

Flast, who had been exhausted by their earlier conversation, jerked awake. 'Destroy Earth?' she said, rubbing her eyes. I don't think they'll need to go that far.' Slowly she stood up and stretched. 'Disrupting it would be enough. During the confusion they would invade, thereby preventing the battle which destroyed their planet.'

The Time Lord's blood was on the verge of congealing, which forced him into a manic session of running on the spot. 'Even to disrupt Earth,' he panted, 'would require a very large bomb.'

'They have a natural one. In fact it's heading to Earth at this very moment.'

Steam now billowed from the Time Lord, like a well-exercised horse on a frosty morning. 'A natural one?' He paused in his exercise, realising what she meant. 'Halley's Comet?'

She nodded. 'They intend to divert it. Cause it to crash into Earth.' Unable to help herself, Flast smiled. 'It will make a very loud bang,' she grinned.

But the Doctor wasn't in the mood for jokes. 'It will do more than that,' he said sternly. 'It will bring about a massive change in established history...' He paused, wondering why the High Council on Gallifrey wasn't doing anything about it. They must have received my distress call, he thought. At least made tentative enquiries as to its source. Even at their laziest, their most decadent, he knew they wouldn't allow a TARDIS to be stolen.

'What are you thinking?' inquired Flast, concerned by his sudden silence.

He sighed. 'Only that the Time Lords don't seem to be doing anything about the Cybermen's activities.'

The Cryon waved a dismissive hand. 'Perhaps their agent is already at work.'

He didn't believe it. 'Then he's taking his time. For a sta –' Again the Doctor froze in mid-word, as a highly depressing thought slipped into his mind. 'Wait a moment,' he murmured. 'It isn't *me?*' Flast peered uncertainly at the Doctor. 'No!' he shouted as though addressing an unseen presence. 'You haven't man-oeuvred me into this mess!' The Doctor paced up and down shaking his fist at the ceiling of his prison. 'It would have helped if you had at least let me know what you intended!'

The Cryon's mouth gaped open. '*You* are a Time Lord?'

'There isn't any need to sound so surprised,' he snapped. 'Especially when I'm feeling so angry.'

'Angry or not, I might be able to help you.' Staggering to a box on the far side of the room, she pulled off its already-unfastened lid. 'It took me days to open this,' she said, remembering the pain of her effort. 'And even then I couldn't do anything with it.'

The Doctor peered inside. 'What is it?' he asked, tentively scooping a little white powder onto his finger.

'Vastial!' He had not heard the name before. 'It's a mineral common in the colder areas of Telos. Not only is it very unstable...' The Doctor rubbed it between his thumb and forefinger, feeling its rough uneven texture. '... but you have enough on your fingers to blow your hand off.' Frantically brushing his hands free of the powder, he gave Flast a particularly sour look. 'Though at this temperature,' she continued sadly, 'it is quite useless.'

Otherwise the Cybermen wouldn't have locked us up with it, he thought. The Doctor now felt foolish for not realising this sooner. 'How hot does it have to get before it becomes unfriendly?'

Flast puckered her lips as she thought for a moment, and not coming to any real conclusion she simply shrugged. 'Unfortunately I am not a scientist,' she said carefully, 'therefore I can't be certain. But I hear that ten degrees above zero is enough – fifteen and it self-ignites.'

'Are you certain?'

She was.

Much to Flast's consternation, a huge smile spread across the Time Lord's face. He patted his pocket and felt the friendly bulge of the sonic device nestling within. Suddenly after so many disappointments, it seemed that the situation might turn to his advantage.

Stratton and Bates rushed along the ducting, their tireless limbs carrying them faster and further than Lytton and Griffiths could manage without pausing to rest.

'How much further?' demanded Stratton.

Lytton consulted a plan displayed on the tiny screen. 'Not far,' he said between laboured gasps for breath.

They continued to jog until they reached a vertical shaft of ducting. Bates glance upwards into the gloom. Built into the wall, and extending as far as he could see, was a ladder. 'Up there?'

Lytton nodded. Bates leapt for the first wrung, caught it, and effortlessly pulled himself up.

'I'll take the gun,' said Lytton, holding out his hand. Stratton wasn't certain. 'I want to act as rear guard while you climb,' he said indignantly. 'If you don't trust me now then we're all doomed.'

Reluctantly Stratton handed over the Cyber gun. In exchange, Lytton gave him the plan. 'Now move!'

Like monkeys, Griffith and Stratton swung up onto the ladder and rapidly started to climb.

Aching from the effort of the run, Lytton leaned against the wall for a moment's rest. Staring into the gloom, back along the ducting they had just travelled, he was pleased to see that it was quiet and deserted. Unfortunately he did not look up at the ceiling above his head. There he would have noticed a tiny lens recording his every movement. This was one of many cameras which had monitored their presence since entering Cyber Control.

Lytton glanced up the horizontal ducting and saw that the ungainly shape of Charlie Griffiths had almost reached the top of the ladder. Taking a last look around, Lytton shouldered the gun and reached for the first wrung. As he did so, a metallic hand came from nowhere, grabbed his leg and savagely pulled him down.

Charlie heard a man scream and looked down.

'There's nothing we can do,' urged Bates, stretching out a helping hand.

Below, in the gloom, Charlie could see the spread-eagled shape of Lytton surrounded by Cybermen. Although he had never liked him, the last thing he would have wished on his worst enemy was being turned into a Cyberman.

Completing his climb, Charlie glanced below once more and saw the Cybermen dragging Lytton to his feet. A moment later he had been taken away.

Stratton indicated that they move off. Reluctantly Charlie followed. He had been paid two million pounds to look after Lytton, but when the crunch actually came, was unable to do anything. This depressed him even more.

If he had been less upset, less tired, less pre-occupied with his own sense of failure, he might have stopped to consider why the Cybermen seemed no longer interested in them.

Instead they ran blindly on...

Flast handed the Doctor her cup and he filled it with a

tiny amount of vastial. Crossing to the door, he took out his sonic lance and pressed it against the control panel. A moment later it was open and the Time Lord was rummaging amongst the wiring inside. Fascinated, the Cryon watched the Doctor at work.

'Are you certain the vastial will explode on contact with the warmer air outside?'

'Certainly within a few seconds,' she said.

Completing his work, he placed his sonic lance on a tiny diode. All he now required to open the door was to pass a pulse of energy between its two electrodes. 'Wait a moment,' he said, looking over his shoulder at the Cryon. 'If I open this door what will happen to you? You can't leave here. The warmth in the corridor will kill you.'

But Flast wasn't interested in such considerations. 'First destroy the guard in the corridor, then we'll discuss it!'

Her tone convinced the Doctor that this was not the time to argue. Activating the diode, the heavy door glided slowly open. He slid the cup containing the vastial onto the corridor.

As it slithered across the floor, the Cyber guard lumbered towards it. Unsuspectingly, he bent to pick it up. At the same moment there was a blinding flash and an enormous explosion. Instantly the Cyberman disintegrated.

Once the smoke had cleared, the Doctor popped his head around the door for a quick inspection. 'When the Cyber Controller learns about this,' he said, withdrawing into the refrigerated area, 'he'll have you killed.'

Flast lowered herself onto a seat near the box of open vastial. 'They'll simply complete a job they started a long time ago,' she muttered pragmatically. 'But now I have a way of fighting them.'

She held out her hand indicating the sonic lance. The Doctor handed it to her. 'This is what I have been waiting for, Time Lord.' She waved an arm at the boxes stacked around them. 'There is enough explosive here to annihilate Cyber Control.'

Although he couldn't dispute the destructive potential, he was very doubtful about the detonator she wished to use. 'There isn't much power left in the lance,' he said. 'And the vastial is very cold. It may not generate enough heat.'

'That is for me to risk.' She held up the lance in a gesture of victory. 'Go, Doctor – we both have important work to do.'

The Time Lord nodded, aware that it was pointless to argue. 'Good luck!' He gave the Cryon greeting and left.

Flast switched on the lance and buried it in the open box of vastial. Carefully she replaced the lid, stood up and moved away. She did not intend to draw attention to it when the Cybermen arrived. Quietly she began to hum a Cryon death lament. If the lance worked the Cybermen would never leave Telos, though she knew it would cost her her life.

On hearing of Lytton's capture, the Cryons had become uneasy. Whereas they knew that Stratton, Bates and Charlie Griffiths were continuing their attempt to steal the Cybermen's time vessel, they also knew they must act concerning the Doctor's TARDIS.

Peri had protested, saying that she did not know how to operate the controls. But the Cryons were adamant that she try. So it was with some forcefulness that she had been ushered to where the TARDIS stood.

But outside stood two Cyber guards. Although they would be easy to destroy, the Cryons did not know how many were inside. Neither could they enter the warm atmosphere of the time machine to find out.

They would have to wait and watch until they could think of some way of solving the problem.

Peri silently prayed that the Doctor would escape and come to their aid.

9

Caught

Dwarfing all around him, the Cyber Controller stood well over two metres high. With legs slightly apart and hands on hips he appeared like a mighty Colossus dominating the middle of the room. Surrounded by counsellors and guards, who fussed and responded to his every need, he made an impressive and terrifying sight.

As Lytton was dragged into his presence, the coterie surrounding the Controller silently turned to face him. 'You have wasted both my time and energy.' Although deeper and richer in tone, the Controller's voice still had the cold, emotionless quality germane to all Cybermen.

Lytton stared defiantly at him, knowing that whatever he said would not prevent his ultimate fate – being turned into a Cyberman.

With far more grace and control than would have been expected from someone as large as the Controller, he glided across the floor to Lytton. 'I know that you planned to steal my time vessel,' he boomed. 'You will tell me how it is to be done.' Lytton felt the gaze of everyone in the room boring into him. 'Well?'

He didn't reply.

The Controller nodded, and two Cybermen flanking Lytton grabbed his hands and slowly started to squeeze. At first he was able to control the pain, but as their grip tightened Lytton began to scream. Those around him looked on, unaffected by his agony. Unable to accept any more pain, he begged for mercy, agreeing to tell them everything they wanted to know.

The Cybermen released his now-bloody hands and he collapsed to the floor. The Controller edged forward and waited for Lytton to speak. Once he had started it was difficult to make him stop. He told them about the Doctor, how he had been stranded on Earth, and the deal he had made with the Cryons. He told them how they planned to steal the time vessel and where they would take it. He told them about Stratton and Bates, and how the Cryons had encouraged them to escape. He told them everything.

Satisfied it was the truth, the Cyber Controller prodded him gently with his foot. 'You are a fool, Lytton,' he declared. 'You could have saved yourself pain by telling us everything when first asked.' Lytton's only reply was a groan. 'Now you will become as we are.'

Lytton was pulled to his feet and taken to one of a row of conversion cabinets. Deftly he was strapped into place and the silver skullcap that would condition his mind was lowered into place. Everyone in the room watched.

'Excellent,' said the Controller. 'Now bring the Doctor to me. He too will become as we are.'

Obeying, a Cyberman spoke urgently into a microphone, but there wasn't any reply. He then pressed a button and the open door to the refrigeration plant, where the Doctor had been held prisoner, flashed up onto a screen. In the foreground of the picture could be seen the destroyed Cyberman.

'The Doctor has escaped!' roared the Controller. 'He must be found!'

There was a great bustle in the room as switches were pressed and guards called to action. Somewhere in the distance a klaxon started to sound. A bleary-eyed Lytton stared out at the busy room. The drugs had already started to affect his mind. He felt strangely calm. Even his hands had stopped hurting. He knew that soon he would be a Cyberman. As this thought began to slowly permeate his fuddled mind, his urge to resist returned. So did the pain: Lytton started to scream.

The Time Lord ran along a huge, desolate gallery that seemed to go on forever. What had once been the neat, ordered resting place for thousands of hibernating Cybermen was now derelict. Doors of many individual tombs had been smashed open. Damaged corpses of Cybermen, some with head and arms missing, littered the floor. Whatever the Cryons had used to poison their life-support system, thought the Doctor, it certainly had had a very odd effect. Instead of killing them outright, many had woken with their brains affected by the drug. This had caused them to smash out of their tombs and attack anything they met.

Although the Cyber Controller had worked hard to locate the source of poisoning, and discover an antidote, he had been unsuccessful. With only a few hundred surviving Cybermen, the future of their race was uncertain. Unable to breed, they relied on converting suitable captives. With so few Cybermen to raid it was simply a matter of time before they ceased to exist.

That was unless the Cyber Controller could change history.

The Doctor leapt over a decaying Cyberman and rounded a corner. A little way ahead was the corridor containing his TARDIS. Skidding to a halt on the frosty floor, he peered into the corridor and saw the mighty portal that was his TARDIS. Standing in front of it was a Cyber guard.

He withdraw his head and considered what to do next. As he pondered, the door of a tomb behind him slowly opened. A moment later, something was prodded into his back. Raising his hands, the Doctor turned and found that he was staring into the barrel of a Cyber gun. Holding it was Varne.

'How do you do,' he said nervously. 'I'm the Doctor.'

'Unless you help us, you won't be for very much longer.' Her voice was without humour.

From behind Varne, inside the tomb, the Doctor heard the concerned voice of Peri call. 'You must help them, Doctor, otherwise they will destroy the TARDIS.' Followed by Rost and two other Cryons, she emerged from the tomb and embraced him. 'Am I pleased to see you,' she said with enormous relief. 'I was afraid you were dead.'

He smiled and gave her a friendly squeeze. 'You don't get rid of me so easily,' he smirked. The Doctor then turned to Varne. 'Now why do you wish to destroy my TARDIS?'

'It would be more accurate to say that we do not wish the Cybermen to control it.'

That much he could agree with. 'How many Cybermen are inside?'

'We have no way of telling.'

'Then we must find out.'

The Doctor peered into the tomb behind Peri, but its occupier had long gone. He then moved along the gallery until he came to a tomb with a sealed door. Summoning up all his strength, the Time Lord threw himself against it, but all he managed to do was bruise his shoulder.

Rost stepped forward. 'Allow me,' she said, producing a hook-like device. Inserting it into a small slot at the side of the door, she gave it a sharp twist. Slowly it slid open to reveal the hibernating Cyberman.

Feeling a little embarrassed by his empty display of machismo, the Doctor thanked her. He then eased his way into the tomb and started to dismantle the dead Cyberman's face-plate. Fortunately time and corrosion had done most of the work for him.

'What are you doing?' asked Peri.

'Cybermen have an inbuilt distress signal.'

'But that thing is dead.'

He nodded. 'Then it's a good thing the signal is electronic and not organic.'

With the face-plate removed, the Doctor began to tear out the banks of micro-electronics. He then scooped out the decomposed remains of the Cyberman's brain, revealing the tiny circuit he was looking for. 'Now,' he muttered, searching for its switch, 'if there is enough residual power...' He flicked it. 'You might just transmit.'

They waited and watched, but nothing happened.

As usual, Peri was confused. 'What are you trying to achieve?'

The Doctor stared nervously at the distress beacon. 'A reaction from inside the TARDIS. Cybermen have one weakness: they will react to the distress of their own kind.'

The Doctor pushed past the Cryons and popped his head into the corridor where the TARDIS was parked. Much to his delight he saw two Cybermen emerging from the time machine. His trick had worked!

'Ready or not,' he whispered to Rost, 'here they come.'

Rost rapidly barked out her orders and the Cryons dispersed along the gallery, hiding in open tombs, their guns ready for action. The Doctor and Peri followed, lodging themselves with Rost.

'How many Cybermen are there?' she asked.

'Two plus the original guard.'

As they silently waited, frost began to settle on them. The atmosphere was tense and Peri was convinced that her pounding heart could be heard the length of the gallery.

Suddenly two Cybermen lumbered into the corridor and the Cryons opened fire. The red-hot beams from the laser guns tore into their metal bodies. A moment later they exploded. Varne let out a cheer and ran forward. But before she could reach the smouldering remains of the first Cyberman, the Cyber guard appeared. Caught without cover, Varne started to fire wildly, but the guard was more accurate. As the energy from his gun hit her, Varne's body vaporised. Immediately the remaining Cryons returned fire and the guard was destroyed.

Rost glared at the Doctor. 'Please remove your TARDIS from Telos,' she said sternly, 'before you need rescuing again.'

He nodded, then indicated a greasy stain, all that remained of Varne. 'Sorry about your friend,' he said.

'Just go, Doctor.'

'And what about you?'

'We shall survive.'

Escorted by Rost, the Doctor and Peri made their way back to the TARDIS. 'I promise you won't see me or the TARDIS again.' The Time Lord raised his hand in a Cryon greeting. 'Come along, Peri.'

'What about Lytton?' Puzzled, he paused.

'Lytton's been captured by the Cybermen,' she exclaimed.

'Then he should be happy.'

'You don't understand.' Peri was becoming agitated. 'Lytton's working for the Cryons! He always has been.'

The Doctor was stunned, but Rost confirmed that it was true.

'You can't leave him to die,' urged Peri.

Neither did the doctor particularly want to tangle with Lytton again. He thought for a moment then turned to Rost. 'Where is Lytton likely to be?'

'Last reports say that he is in the laboratory of the Cyber Controller.'

'All right,' he said after a long pause, 'I'll see what I can do.'

Rost gave a funny little bow. 'We are grateful, Time Lord.'

'Oh, by the way,' he said, pushing open the TARDIS door, 'you'd better get your people away from here.'

Rost didn't understand.

'While I was a prisoner I met a friend of yours.'

The Cryon thought for a moment. 'Flast?' He nodded. 'But we thought she was dead.'

'She soon will be: she intends to explode a room full of vastial.'

Grabbing Peri by the arm, he pushed her into the

TARDIS. 'Good luck.'

Again Rost saluted.

Once inside the TARDIS, the Doctor set to work calculating the precise position of the Cyber Controller's laboratory. Although he was getting quite good at controlling the erratic nature of the TARDIS, all it would require would be one small miscalculation and the time machine would materialise inside a wall. The last time this happened it had taken him nearly five days to extricate himself. As Flast was desperate to set off her bomb, the Doctor was aware it was an error best not made.

A Cyber Leader with an escort of three Cybermen entered the refrigeration unit where Flast was held prisoner.

'Search the room,' ordered the Cyber Leader. 'The Time Lord may have set a trap using the vastial.'

Immediately the Cybermen started their hunt. Flast watched as they searched dangerously near to the box with the sonic lance.

'You!' called the Cyber Leader. 'Come here.' Slowly Flast limped towards him. 'How long ago did the Time Lord escape?' She shrugged; but the Leader wasn't prepared to accept such casualness and viciously grabbed her by the neck. 'Answer my question!' he demanded.

Flast gagged as the collar of her tunic bit into her skin. 'Don't know,' she choked. 'Don't have an instrument for measuring time.'

The Cyberman remained dogmatic. 'You will answer my question.'

'I cannot!'

Unimpressed by her excuses, he lifted her clear of the ground and hurled her across the room like a ragdoll. 'Did the Time Lord open any of the vastial boxes?' Stunned by her fall, Flast was unable to reply. 'Take her outside,' ordered the Leader.

Like a bundle of dirty washing, Flast was picked up and carried into the warm corridor. Dumping her on the ground, the Cyberman moved back to the doorway where the Cyber Leader was waiting.

'You still have a few moments to change you mind,' he said.

Flast didn't speak or move, but lay where she had been thrown. But as the warmth of the corridor began to penetrate her tunic, so did the pain. At first it felt like sharp needles pricking at her skin. As the temperature rose, the sensation changed to that of boiling water. It was then that Flast began to scream. As she blindly dragged herself back to the safety of the refrigeration room, steam began to pour from her body – she was beginning literally to melt. Digging nails hard into the floor, she struggled on until her path was blocked by the legs of the Cyber Leader. Unable to beat her way past this metal barrier, she slowly died where she lay.

As the Cyber Leader turned back into the refrigeration room, he noticed burn marks next to the door control panel. He examined them carefully and realised they had been made by a sonic lance. When he reported this to the Controller he destroyed the Cyberman who had imprisoned the Doctor without first searching him. He ordered extra squads to help search the refrigeration area, knowing that if the lance was not found, it meant the end of Cyber Control.

*

A heavy metal door barred their way. Bates checked the electronic plan. 'The launch pad for the time vessel should be on the other side,' he said.

'We've made it then!' crowed Stratton.

Charlie Griffiths felt like being more cautious. 'Let's get aboard the ship before we celebrate.'

The others knew his was the more sensible attitude, but their excitement was beginning to affect their judgement.

'Right,' said Bates. 'How do we get this door open?' He gave it a kick, but instead of the dull thud of metal there was an explosion. Bates was killed instantly. Stratton and Charlie turned to run, but through the smoking remains of the door, came several pencil-thin beams from a laser gun.

They collapsed, both dead before their bodies hit the ground.

A Cyberman stepped into the ducting to confirm that his handiwork had been satisfactorily completed. When he turned Griffiths over with his foot, he found that the Earthman had a wry smile on his face.

To lose is always to lose. But to nearly win, as Charlie and the others had done, always offers some satisfaction. The Cyberman who stared down at Charlie could not understand this nor appreciate the significance of the smile. To the Cyberman, winning was the only thing; to lose was failure. But any social structure that lacked all feeling and culture was already losing: the irony was lost on Charlie's murderer.

Charlie Griffiths had not led a particularly good life. Until he had met Lytton, neither had he been very successful. But in all his wildest dreams he never believed that he would die on an alien planet with two million pounds' worth of uncut diamonds in his pocket. He hadn't wanted to die, but whatever else could be said, he had done so in some style.

10

The Final Encounter

Commander Gustave Lytton stared out at the empty room. Although his vision was distorted and his mind confused, he was convinced he could see a blue flickering blob. With enormous effort he attempted to focus his eyes. As the edges of the blur began to harden, his ears were suddenly full of a loud noise and Lytton thought he was hallucinating, especially when he saw a blue police box materialise in the corner of the room. Suddenly its door was thrown open and the familiar shape of the Doctor appeared. Lytton blinked. 'I know you,' he muttered.

'That's right,' said the Time Lord, as he raced across the room. 'What's more, I'm just beginning to find out about you.'

The Doctor started to detach the silver skullcap as Lytton began to cough. 'Did you put the sonic lance to good use?' he gasped.

The Doctor nodded. 'But why didn't you tell me what you were up to?'

'Too late now.' Confusion was again beginning to take hold of his mind. 'Now you must kill.'

'Oh no.' The Doctor continued to struggle with the skullcap, but was finding it difficult to detach the tubing. 'I can help you . . . Just hang on.'

Looking round for something sharp, the Doctor saw a heavy knife on a work bench. Quickly he fetched it and started to hack his way through the tubing.

'I did my best . . .' Lytton moaned. 'Kept my word.'

'I know.'

As he spoke, he heard a door slide open behind him. Glancing over his shoulder, the Time Lord saw the Cyber Controller, gun in hand, entering the room.

'Move away from him,' he intoned.

Surreptitiously the Doctor slipped the knife into Lytton's hand, then did as instructed.

Noticing the disconnected tubing, the Cyber Controller moved to correct the damage. 'Emotion is a weakness,' he said.

The Doctor was sceptical. 'Oh, I don't know.'

'It brought you back for your friend, and therefore your death.'

As the Controller inspected the damage, Lytton summoned up his last reserves of strength and attempted to drive the knife into his respirator. But such was the thickness of metal, it harmlessly skidded across its surface. Lytton stabbed again, and this time caught a hydraulic line near the top of the Controller's arm. Pressing with all his might, he twisted and turned the knife, until he finally managed to rupture it. Green fluid spurted from the wound, causing the arm to go into spasm, and the Controller to drop his gun. Lytton, exhausted by his efforts, collapsed into unconsciousness. With his damaged arm now under control, the Cyber Controller turned on Lytton, raised his good arm and, with a mighty blow across his neck, killed him.

Seeing his chance, the Doctor snatched up the dropped gun. As he did so, two Cybermen entered the room. Quickly he threw himself onto the floor, firing as he fell. Luck was on his side. The laser beams from his gun tore into the leading Cyberman. As he collapsed, the Doctor fired again and the second Cyberman was destroyed.

Roaring like a wild animal, and slashing at the air with his fist, the Controller ran at the Time Lord. Holding up the gun, and using it like a quarterstaff, the Doctor managed to parry the killer blows and struggle to his feet. The Controller continued to chop savagely and wildly, catching him several painful blows. The furious onslaught prevented the Doctor from manipulating his gun into the firing position. What was more, the blows he had received, and the effort of fighting, were beginning to exhaust him.

The Controller continued to press home his ruthless attack, forcing the Doctor to retreat across the room and into a corner. Seeing his prey was trapped, the Controller momentarily paused before delivering his death blow. The Doctor watched as the mighty fist was driven down towards him. Blindly he leapt to one side, the fist missing by millimetres. The effort behind the attack caused the Controller to overbalance. This was what the Doctor had been waiting for, as it gave him the vital seconds to level his gun. He fired angrily, aggressively, repeatedly. The Cyber Controller staggered. Then his enormous frame exploded.

Discarding the gun, the Time Lord lurched exhaustedly to where Lytton lay. Peri, who had been watching the fight on the scanner inside the TARDIS, ran from the time machine and attempted to grab hold of him. 'There's nothing you can do, Doctor.'

'I've got to help him,' he protested.

Peri could see from the dreadful angle of Lytton's head that it was useless. 'It's too late,' she pleaded, 'he's dead!' Both physically and emotionally exhausted, the Time Lord didn't want to believe what he was told. 'There's absolutely nothing you can do,' Peri repeated attempting to steer the Doctor back towards the TARDIS.

He glanced back at Lytton's body then reluctantly allowed himself to be led inside. 'Why didn't he say something?' he muttered.

Peri closed the door of the TARDIS and a few moments later the time machine dematerialised.

Strict logic and lack of empathy had always restricted the Cybermen's ability to think laterally. This occasion was no exception. Believing that to hide something well meant burying it, they had wasted valuable time pulling down and searching the enormous stacks of vastial boxes. It did not for a moment occur to them that the one left casually in a dark shadow could contain the sonic lance.

While they searched, the device had done its work. Slowly it warmed the chemical, raising the temperature to above zero.

It wasn't until a Cyberman picked up the box that he noticed it was smoking. But it was all too late. As he ripped off the lid the vastial flashed, then exploded. Acting as a perfect detonator, its violent eruption set off the remaining boxes, creating an enormous fireball which tore its angry way through Cyber Control, destroying everything in its path. It travelled on into the tombs terminating the lives of the few surviving Cybermen in hibernation. Then as an encore it raised its voice in a mighty roar which ripped apart the fabric of the buildings.

Deep in the caves stood Rost and the other Cryons listening intently to the explosion. For them the flames were purifying and cleansing, destroying the thing they hated most. The Cybermen on Telos were all dead. Now they could get on with rebuilding their planet.

The Doctor leaned against the console, and for a full minute, watched the time rotor oscillate. 'Didn't go very well, did it?' he said at last.

Peri shrugged. 'Earth's safe. So is the Web of Time.'

He turned to face his companion. 'I didn't mean it like that.'

Wanting to comfort him Peri smiled and took his hand. 'I know. But there was little you could do for him. It wasn't that he didn't have the opportunity to tell you.'

Sighing he moved away from Peri. 'He didn't tell me,' he said, categorically, 'because he knew I wouldn't believe him... To be honest, I don't think I've ever misjudged anyone quite as badly as I did Lytton.'

Peri watched as he left the console room slamming the door behind him. She wanted to follow and comfort him, but knew it would be pointless.

So this is the new Doctor, she thought. Wild and unpredictable; patronising and egotistical; yet at the same time able to display compassion, something she had never seen him do before. Peri decided that was an improvement. Whether she could live as happily with the other aspects of his new personality, only time would tell...

DOCTOR WHO

	TERRANCE DICKS	
0426114558	**Doctor Who –** **Abominable Snowmen**	£1.35
0426203054	**Doctor Who–Ambassadors** **of Death**	£1.95
0426200373	**Doctor Who – Android Invasion**	£1.25
0426201086	**Doctor Who – Androids of Tara**	£1.95
0426193423	**Doctor Who – Arc of Infinity**	£1.35
0426202538	PAUL ERIKSON **Dr Who – The Ark**	£1.75
0426116313	IAN MARTER **Doctor Who – Ark in Space**	£1.95
0426201043	TERRANCE DICKS **Doctor Who –** **Armageddon Factor**	£1.50
0426112954	**Doctor Who – Auton Invasion**	£1.50
0426201582	ERIC PRINGLE **Doctor Who – The Awakening**	£1.50
0426195884	JOHN LUCAROTTI **Doctor Who – The Aztecs**	£1.50
0426202546	TERENCE DUDLEY **Dr Who – Black Orchid**	£1.75
042620123X	DAVID FISHER **Doctor Who –** **Creature from the Pit**	£1.95
0426113160	DAVID WHITAKER **Doctor Who – Crusaders**	£1.50
0426116747	TERRANCE DICKS **Doctor Who – Brain of Morbius**	£1.95
0426110250	**Doctor Who –** **Carnival of Monsters**	£1.50*

DOCTOR WHO

0426193261	CHRISTOPHER H. BIDMEAD **Doctor Who – Castrovalva**	£1.50
0426199596	TERRANCE DICKS **Doctor Who – The Caves of Androzani**	£1.50
042611471X	MALCOLM HULKE **Doctor Who – Cave Monsters**	£1.50
0426202511	G. DAVIS & A. BINGEMAN **Dr Who – The Celestial Toymaker**	£1.60
0426117034	TERRANCE DICKS **Doctor Who – Claws of Axos**	£1.50
0426114981	BRIAN HAYLES **Doctor Who – Curse of Peladon**	£1.50
0426114639	GERRY DAVIS **Doctor Who – Cybermen**	£1.50
0426113322	BARRY LETTS **Doctor Who – Daemons**	£1.50
0426101103	DAVID WHITAKER **Doctor Who – Daleks**	£1.50
042611244X	TERRANCE DICKS **Doctor Who – Dalek Invasion of Earth**	£1.50
0426103807	**Doctor Who – Day of The Daleks**	£1.35
0426119657	**Doctor Who – Deadly Assassin**	£1.50
042620042X	**Doctor Who – Death to The Daleks**	£1.35
0426200969	**Doctor Who – Destiny of the Daleks**	£1.50

ORDER FORM

STAR BOOKS are obtainable from many booksellers and newsagents. If you have any difficulty list the titles you want and fill in the form below:

TITLE   PRICE

_____

_____

_____

_____

_____

_____

Name _____

Address _____

_____

Send to: Star Books Cash Sales, P.O. Box 11, Falmouth, Cornwall, TR10 9EN.

Please send a cheque or postal order to the value of the cover price plus: UK: 55p for the first book, 22p for the second book and 14p for each additional book ordered to the maximum charge of £1.75.

BFPO and EIRE: 55p for the first book, 22p for the second book, 14p per copy for the next 7 books, thereafter 8p per book.

OVERSEAS: £1.00 for the first book and 25p per copy for each additional book.

While every effort is made to keep prices low, it is sometimes necessary to increase prices at short notice. Star Books reserve the right to show new retail prices on covers which may differ from those advertised in the text or elsewhere.

*NOT FOR SALE IN CANADA